JEREMIAH WASH: THE GREY

B.E. Amestoy

JEREMIAH WASH: THE GREY

ACKNOWLEDGMENTS:

This book, *Jeremiah Wash: The Grey*, originally started out as the back story for a character in a tabletop RPG myself and some friends would play. The game was invented by a gentleman I only had the pleasure of meeting a few brief times.

After beginning this book, the group I played with had a slight falling out, yet I still felt as I should complete the story I had begun. Because of this, I changed many of the main plot points in the story so it would not interfere with the story they had created in their game. I would have liked to include many other details within these pages to acknowledge their creative minds, yet found it best to eliminate any mention all together.

Still, I would like to thank them for the inspiration and the good times we shared around that kitchen table in a small cramped apartment that we would play in. The few brews, the hot tea, the laughs and tears.

As a special thank you to the reader for purchasing this book, I have included the original short story that inspired the book titled *Jeremiah Wash*.

I hope you enjoy!

Also, a special thank you to my mother, who spent hours combing through the book as my "editor" before print. Thank you, mom!

Cheers!

-    B. E. Amestoy

The Stuart Highway felt as if it were never ending, spectacularly desolate in the mid-morning sun. She looked out her windshield, taking in the long stretch of flat nothingness before her; one ebony arm hung out the driver's window as her hand began to pat the side of the truck to the beat of the music. A dust storm from the day before left a fine red film to cover her forty-three-meter-long road train. The windshield streaked from a less than spectacular washing job, leaving the red mud caked under the windshield wipers. However, this didn't concern her; she just wanted to finish her run and have a long rest, maybe a pint somewhere if she could. Afterwards, she would address the filth that covered her vehicle.

Got a storm coming in from the top end, a voice came over her radio, *look out for yourselves, its looking like a-*

The radio shut off, her engine began to sputter and spit; no power. "Shit" she muttered under her breath as she did her best to guide the road train off to the long paddock. It finally came to a complete stop after a couple hundred meters, allowing her to exit and take a look at what happened. She recoiled as black smoke billowed out of the engine, blocking her sight from whatever gremlin caused her unwanted stop.

"Wanker," She sighed under her breath as she rubbed her forehead; not a good time to be breaking down in the middle of the Outback. The temperature had already reached about 36 degrees, causing her to sweat under the sun. *But how did I break down,* she thought to herself, *just had work done three days ago.* Her eyes met the horizon, searching for any approaching vehicles to flag down. From the south, there was nothing, just the stretching road dotted with red, brown, and scattered green.

Suddenly, the truck roared to life on its own accord. She stood there, shocked and stunned, unable to figure out what may have happened. She looked at the engine, nothing seemed to be out of place or broken. As far as she could tell nothing should have caused the engine to die. She closed the bonnet before climbing back into her cab, checking all the gauges; everything was normal.

Before she could switch it into gear, she looked up, seeing a blackened cloud rolling over the hood of her truck.

SYSTEM CHECK…

ELECTRICITY LEVELS... 3 PERCENT BELOW OPTIMAL PERFORMANCE...

HEART RATE... 60BPM...

SIGHT... LOADING... LOADING... MAINTENANCE REQUIRED...

MUSCLE CONTRACTION... NORMAL...

MEMORY BOOT... 18 PERCENT UNOBTAINABLE... CORRUPT FILES PROCESSED... CORRUPT FILES DELETED... OPTIMAL MEMORY SPACE RESTORED...

SIGHT... LOADING... LOADING... MAINTENANCE REQUIRED...

TRANSMITTER... LOADING... LOADING... 5 PERCENT BELOW OPTIMAL PERFORMANCE...

MOVEMENT... NORMAL...

AIR FILTRATION... OPTIMAL PERFORMANCE...

REFLEXES... 9 PERCENT BELOW OPTIMAL PERFORMANCE... MAINTENANCE REQUIRED...

SIGHT REBOOT... REBOOT... REBOOT...

SIGHT OPERATING AT OPTIMAL LEVELS...

SYSTEM BOOT COMPLETE...

WAKING... WAKING... WAKING...

He awoke among deteriorating trees and brush within a small crater caused by his fall from orbit. His hand began to move with mechanical whirl as the words *INITIATIVE DOWNLOADING... 3 PERCENT...* flashed with blue hue in his sight. *7 PERCENT...* Commands from his mainframe allowed him to check the status of his 78 percent mechanical body as he rose. His sight was blurred slightly from the information processing before him.

He scanned his surroundings for signs of life in the once luscious New England forest; only small insects remained, and they too were on the brink of extinction. He began a brisk walk up the side of an unfamiliar rotten tail, testing the air as he went. Had he still been able to dream, this would not have been how he envisioned Earth.

OXYGEN 5 PERCENT, POLLUTANTS STILL REMAIN... HABITABILITY; 8 PERCENT... AIR FILTRATION FUNCTIONING AT OPTIMAL LEVELS... REDUCING OXYGEN USE BY 35 PERCENT...

INITIATIVE DOWNLOAD 14 PERCENT...

His mission needed more time to load, but already the outlook was unfavorable. Long ago man had destroyed their home for the lust of technology and progress, causing them to branch out into the cosmic ocean; not out of curiosity, but out of necessity. Humanity's last stand on earth remained with him and the group of scientists who remained in geosynchronous orbit above. Everything he saw, felt, computed, it was all being transmitted up to the station for processing.

INITIATIVE DOWNLOAD 20 PERCENT...

UNKNOWN STORM APPROACHING flashed before his eyes in red, indicating danger, *SPEED AT 35KPH, ADVISE TO AVOID...*

He increased his speed, running from a storm he couldn't see through the dense atmosphere of ancient carbon emissions. *STORM 8 KILOMETERS FROM LOCATION, INCREASING SPEED AT 2KPH PER MINUTE, ADVISE SHUT DOWN TO PROTECT DATA... MISSION TO RESUME ONCE THE STORM PASSES...* His system caused him to freeze in place, shutting down all of his mechanical body except for the download of initiative. His eyes closed as the storm consumed him.

INITIATIVE DOWNLOAD SUSPENDED AT 38 PERCENT... SIGNAL LOST... ADVISE REBOOT...

... ...

REBOOT FAILED...

The Los Angeles streetlights never died; the city shone as another sun at night to lead the chaotic drivers and barflies home. Not for her, these lights lead her from hope to Hell each and every night. She was only five blocks away from her work, and every step slowed as the encroaching weight of dealing with customers came to her mind. Her *SFC* shoes came to a stop, three blocks away from the *Denny's* that provided a way to pay rent. Her shift starts in ten minutes; she could be a few minutes late.

She pulled out a cigarette that she had obtained from a customer a few days before; she knew it would come in handy around finals. Although she never liked to smoke much, the stress had caused her to crack under its pressure. She lit it, savoring the sweet smoke as she exhaled the long grueling day. She knew it wasn't over, but she deserved a break once in a while.

Her blue eyes caught the neon lights, fluorescent bulbs, passing taillights, oncoming headlights; all of it sweeping her over as she sat with her back against some unknown building she had to have passed a million times before. However, at this moment, it was just her and the sweet ember of relaxation. *Do I really want to go into work?* She asked herself as her head lulled back to softly meet the bricks behind her. Her eyes closed for a split second, allowing her to take in the sounds of the city.

The City of Angels... Bullshit...

When her eyes opened once more, she rose to her feet to continue her short commute. After only a block of walking, she noticed a different scent in the air, a different noise casting off from the pavement. Her eyes turned behind her to see a fog colliding with the calm sky over the Los Angeles streets, approaching unchecked by the buildings in its way.

Nuclear fallout is one hell of a thing he read on the walls as he foraged through what once was someone's fallout shelter; someone's home. The bodies lay as if they were sleeping, bones visible through the weak skin and tattered clothing, blood crusted to a black on the grey concrete floor. He found there were no supplies in the lonesome bunker, other than three shots from an old colt revolver and some unusable water.

The one nice thing about the gruesome situation was that he could remove his gas mask, thanks to the disused air filtration system that sputtered to life as he entered the bunker. The stench was next too unbearable from the rotting corpses, but the air was much cleaner than outside. While the gun could have been salvaged, he decided the risk was not worth the reward. He walked around the bodies, doing his best to leave no evidence of his intrusion. He re-positioned his gas mask over his face and began to make his way up to the surface.

Although it was blisteringly hot out in the wasteland, his entire body was covered in thick, mismatched clothing. UV radiation was not something to toy around with, and he knew it. Sweat began to bead within the gasmask, fogging his vision, making him slow his pace to an uncomfortable crawl. Spending too much time out in the wasteland wasn't something anyone really did, but if you didn't move, you died. If you walked too long, you died. If you stayed in a conspicuous building, you died. There was a hell of a lot of ways to die; definitely a hell of a lot more than before the complete nuclear holocaust that swept the world. Some people called it *The Reckoning*, some called it *The Pale Horse*, but he called it by what he felt it really was; *Bullshit Thanks to Politics*.

He was close to his newest hideout, yet he shouldered his old AR 15. There really wasn't anywhere safe, nowhere you could fully let your guard down. Even as he eased his way into the steel enclosure, his gun remained at the ready. There were many times he walked in on some squatters stealing his supplies, and he was already running way too low to lose anything. Thankfully, everything was in place, and no one was hiding in the dark corners. Before he lifted his mask, he knew he had to take a look around the perimeter. It was more out of comfort than necessity, after all, if someone was out there he would have been shot dead before even reaching the door.

He walked out, meeting a blackened grey mist as it crashed into him.

Sweat beaded on her brow, adrenaline coursing through her veins; the stench of pine sap and burnt metal clashed to her nostrils. The sound of the crowd blended perfectly with the echo of cracking bone against her knuckles. Her opponent stumbled backward, reaching up to her nose as blood spewed through the cracks between the fingers. She wanted to breathe for a moment but knew that she couldn't let her opponent regain her footing. Gliding through the air, she decimated the still stumbling opponent with four more blows before watching her fall to a slump on the wood pulp that covered the floor.

She raised her hands in victory as the crowd cheered, spilling beer and wine atop dirtied boots. Someone came to her side, clearing her knuckles of blood, tending to her wounds. She looked over at her downed opponent, seeing spectators scamper over to her, fanning her with shirts and papers.

The cheering slowly became a murmur as more and more of the spectators began to crowd around the downed woman. Someone screamed out in French, another in German. Something had gone terribly wrong. She pushed herself through the crowd, knocking into some with such force they lost their footing to fall face first into the ground. Finally, she reached her opponent; turning cold and blue, eyes pure white as summer clouds. She reached down, shaking her opponent, tears beginning to drown her vision. She screamed out, first in French, then in English; "Ouvre les yeux! Ouvre les yeux! Open your eyes! Wake up! Wake up!"

Her head lulled back as she frantically shook her. Someone placed a hand on her shoulder, only to be greeted by her fist meeting their cheek. She couldn't let her opponent die; it isn't supposed to end like this in a clean fight. More hands reached for her, eventually pulling her from the blue figure. She could see the blood trickling from her nose to the ground, those eyes still unresponsive.

She was pushed out into the New York street, knees crunching against the grey and black snow. "Fumée!" She yelled out to the men who dragged her outside.

Someone relinquished a cigarette, tossing it to her before shutting the door to the red brick warehouse she had been fighting within. She scrambled to light it; her hands shaking with anxiety, grief heavy in her mind. Before she could take her first drag, the streets around her swarmed with a foul smelling smog.

CHAPTER 2

Jeremiah Washington worked on his ranch, providing for his family even during troubling times. When the Civil War broke the country in half, he refused to go into battle and was only willing to pick up a gun in order to defend his own home. And so, he defended his land, his cattle, and his family with ferocity; while still holding his son and wife with the utmost love and respect.

Jeremiah Washington never liked the sound of his last name; to him, it was too prestigious, and he was just a simple man looking to live a very simple life. Any document signed, or formal introduction, he would always use a somewhat simplified version of his name; *Jeremiah Wash*. He preferred it that way; it made him seem more humble in his eyes, and so his wife and his only son went by that simplified last name as well. To those who knew him well, he was just *Jeremiah*, new faces and acquaintances would try to call him *Wash*, sometimes he heard *Mr. Washington*; however, he always corrected them by saying *Jeremiah* with a smile.

His hair was shaggy; the color of straw and always seemed to be a mess. To correct this without the need for grooming each day, he chose to always wear a broad-brimmed brown hat to cover it. That hat also provided him with the much needed personal shade in the hot Texas sun.

Sideburns of the same color framed his face, extending down to the line at which his lips met; thick and scraggly. The sideburns were only there to hide a scar on the left side of his face that he had acquired at a young age while helping his father build a fence. A board slipped from his hands just as he tripped over his foot; slamming his face into the plank and terrifying himself from the blood that seeped onto the ground.

His eyes, deep green in color, pierced through anyone he spoke to, always full of caring, yet intense like the summer sun in Texas. He wasn't the best looking man, but many thought he had kindness in his eyes, loyalty; and so he was viewed as handsome by almost all who met him.

On Sunday mornings, he would wake before his wife and son; groom himself the way he wouldn't any other day, combing his hair to the side, and dress for church. Almost as if instructed, by the time he would finish buttoning his shirt his wife would greet him with a kiss. She would then gather their son and get them both prepared for the thirteen-mile ride into town. She loved him, with all her being, and held their faith as dear as he. She was devoted to him in a way he never dreamed possible.

This was the life of Jeremiah; simple and peaceful, filled with hard work, and faith.

On a Spring day in 1867 Jeremiah had begun his day as usual; waking at dawn to begin work on his ranch. Unfortunately, it had been hard for him to obtain coffee during the Civil War, and so tobacco had to suffice in place of his morning drink for the past couple of years. And although the block had been lifted with the end of the war, he still found it harder to come by than he would have prefered. He did, however, manage to get ahold of some tea just a week before, so this week had been more inviting at the thought of a hot beverage to start each long day with.

Though he did not particularly like tea, he learned to tolerate it. As he waited for a small bit of water to boil over the small stove that sat in the main room of his home, he rolled himself a cigarette with the finest of southern tobacco he had. Although the coffee may have been hard to come by, tobacco was plentiful, even if most of it had to be obtained through trade of his chicken's eggs.

His tea was brewed, his cigarette lit, and now he waited; sitting on an old wooden bucket at the back of his little house. *Not long*, he thought to himself as he sipped the steaming tea. The door creaked open, and his son Robert, who went by Bobby, stumbled out; still putting on one of his boots.

"Is it time, papa?" Bobby said, with an excited yet sleep strewn feel in his voice. He was only seven years old, straw blonde hair like his father, sea blue eyes like his mother. His nose was like a button in between two slightly chubby cheeks that were tanned by his time playing and working in the sun.

"Well," Jeremiah replied, patting his son on the head, "Looks to be about that time. Might want to hurry though, Bobby, those chickens should be wakin' any second." He paused, holding his hand to his ear, "Actually, sounds like they're a stirin' right now. Go on."

Bobby's smile lit up as he ran around to the side of the chicken coop that stood just behind the small house. He unlatched a small compartment and proceeded to pull out a sack of grains, corn, and other items used to feed and care for the chickens. He spread the grains and corn around the front of the coop before placing it back in its compartment and latching it shut. The chickens began to cluck and scratch at the small wooden door. He came back around to the front and opened the little door to allow the chickens to come out as a flood of feathers and dust. "C'mon! C'mon chickitties! Breakfast time!" Bobby called over the heads of the chickens before running back to sit on the ground in front of his father. There, Bobby watched the chickens frantically peck and scratch at the ground where the food had been laid.

Jeremiah smoked and sipped his tea, watching the chickens with his son. He explained to him how he needed to watch the chickens and make sure they didn't run away. "I know that papa!" Bobby would say. Jeremiah knew that Bobby understood this routine by now; Jeremiah would go out and check on the cattle, and Bobby would stay home and tend the chickens as he did his schooling. Today was no exception to this, and soon Jeremiah began to saddle his horse in preparation for his ride out to meet the cattle where he left them the night before.

Before leaving he re-entered his home to gather the rest of his supplies for the day. He was greeted by his wife, who was making breakfast for herself and Bobby. Jennifer was beautiful; long auburn hair caressed her shoulders, blue eyes calm and serene. Her cheeks always appeared to have a reddish glow about them, radiating her kind soul. To him, she was nothing less than perfect. He hugged her from behind and kissed her softly on the cheek. Even without seeing her face he could feel her smile, and she could feel his.

"I love you" she whispered as she nuzzled her head against his.

Jeremiah slowly let go of her, "I love you too." He replied as he made his way out the door once more to ride out into his land. To him, this was always the hardest part of the day, yet he knew it to be absolutely necessary in order to care for his beloved family.

The Sun was already completely over the horizon, though just barely; perfect timing for the ride out on his 150 acres of land to meet up with his cattle. He was prepared, just as always. He carried his Smith & Wesson Model 1 Revolver on his hip. Only a month ago a friend had given him a Winchester Model 1866 as a trade for one of his heads of cattle. He'd grown to appreciate that rifle, and so it was slung across his back, though he knew it would only be used for hunting. He carried a satchel containing a Bible, some food for the day, a small notebook and pen, extra ammunition for both weapons, and a knife. His horse's saddle held small bags containing simple tools, water, and some first aid equipment.

The day was calm; no wind pressed against his face as he met the fence line. What was that different scent in the air? It infected his nostrils, catapulted his brain into a flurry of possibilities; yet none satisfied him. He shook the smell out of his mind and continued to find his way to where he had left his cattle, checking different fence posts as he went along. He had to make sure the fence was still in good condition, as well as make sure no one had entered his land to steal any of his livestock. This was very routine, and he had perfected the art of checking the fence on horseback. This helped to make his day slightly shorter since he didn't have to dismount every couple of posts to check them, but he knew he had not gotten it down to an exact science. Because of this, he knew he had to properly inspect the fence on foot every few weeks, but luckily today was not one of those days.

The scent returned; he halted his horse and sniffed the air. What was it? Where was it coming from? He looked around himself from the saddle; focused on the ground. Nothing. Finally, he rose his eyes to the horizon. There he noticed a thick black fog rolling in quickly from the North-West. He watched, calmly; he had never seen a storm like this in his life, but still he knew he needed to continue with his work. Worse came to worse, he would just be stuck out of his home for the night as he waited for the storm to roll past.

Eventually, he came across a part of the fence where there was some repair needed to a downed board. Luckily for him, it was only a couple hundred yards from where the Cattle were grazing peacefully on the dried grass. Jeremiah dismounted his horse and began to mend the fence the best he could with the limited supplies he had. Suddenly the sun seemed to vanish from the sky. The black mist he had observed earlier descended onto him; that same stench emanating from its vile smoke. The cattle were swallowed up, their sounds ceased as if they were never there at all. Jeremiah rose to his feet; his horse was crying out. He did his best to calm her before mounting her. Unfortunately, it was not enough, and she bucked him off. The last thing he saw was her running into the mist before he slammed against the ground, knocking him out.

Jeremiah awoke in a haze; the mist was stagnant and calm around him. He felt a throbbing in his right leg and looked at it to notice it covered in a crust of blood. He remained calm, studied his surroundings. Nothing seemed to be in sight; the hills, the cattle, the fence, it all seemed to vanish into the vile storm that had descended onto his land. Something caught his eye, and there, only a few feet from him, he saw that his horse had bucked off more than just him. One of the packs from her saddle lay in the dirt only a few yards away. He crawled over; praying silently to himself as the throbbing in his leg worsened by his movements.

Hopefully, it contained his minuscule amount of first aid equipment.

It felt like he crawled for hours; heart pulsing in his ears, blurring his vision on every beat ever so slightly. He reached it; clawing out to drag it toward himself. With shaky hands he reached inside, searching until he breathed a long sigh of relief; his rudimentary supplies were indeed there.

He took a moment to patch himself up before slowly raising to his feet. Using his Winchester as a crutch, he began to make his way in the direction of home. He limped over every patch of grass, every fallen branch. Something was different in the terrain; something different in the air. It was as if the Devil himself had come up from Hell, cascading the world's light into darkness. However, Jeremiah felt that the Devil couldn't even stomach the shit-storm that he was living through; the Devil couldn't breathe the air that now surrounded Jeremiah's head.

Had Jeremiah sinned? Did he really deserve this?

Finally, after miles of stumbling, he could make out the silhouette of his little house. His heart began to pound; he was *finally* home. He fell down to his knees, slinging his Winchester to his back, he began to crawl as fast as he could towards the small beacon of hope.

Before he could reach the front door, he noticed his horse dead just off to the right side of his porch. She had been ripped to shreds as if a pack of wolves had apprehended her in the safety of his land. He held his mouth, attempting to keep his bowels inside as they churned and began to make him heave. Then, it all settled as his heart dropped; he saw a trail of blood leading into his house.

Quickly he retrieved his rifle from his back; using it as a cane as he hobbled inside and drew his pistol. The front room was destroyed, nothing remained in place. The stove seemed to have been ripped up and thrown across the room, chairs and books chaotically scattered over the floor. He stepped lightly over the crumpled paper and debris as best he could, keeping his sights down the barrel of his pistol. He looked to the door, following the blood that trailed into his room. The old doorframe had deep scratches and a light mist of blood, the door hanging slightly by one hinge.

He crept through the door, and nearly broke down into tears as his left heel thudded against the creaking wood; there on the floor was his beloved Jennifer with her stomach torn out through her mouth. Her entrails were left laying behind her head, blood soaking into the floor. Her blue eyes still wide open, staring into his soul.

Bobby kneeled over his mother; his back to the door. Jeremiah dropped to his knees and began to crawl to his son. His rifle was left leaning on the door frame. He didn't know what to say, how would he comfort his poor son? He pushed these thoughts aside as he reached his hand out to pat his son on the back. Before he could open his mouth to comfort him, Bobby turned around to face his father; blood and viscera oozing from between his teeth. His blue eyes were gone, only green and red consuming the iris', his pupils slit as a cat; they locked onto him, wide and destroying. Bobby leaped towards his father; mouth open as an animal on the attack. His teeth sank into his father's right leg just where he had dressed his wound, taking a small chunk of flesh out of it.

Jeremiah's pistol flew from his hands in the brief scuffle. He attempted to reach for it, but his son was right on top of him; hissing, coughing, biting at the air as Jeremiah lifted his right forearm against Bobby's chest to prevent him from reaching his face. He reached with his left hand for the pistol, clawing at the floor; he was only a few inches away. He couldn't reach the pistol. Jeremiah began to think of his life and how he'd ended up here. The foul stench returned to his nostrils, his body forced him to cough in protest; Bobby's face kept getting closer and closer. He pushed with all of his might and was able to turn over his son. Jeremiah put his hand around Bobby's neck, but Bobby kept biting and clawing at the air; reaching for his father's face.

Jeremiah reached to his right, grabbing his Winchester as he kicked his son off of him. In one fluid motion, he said a prayer and put a bullet in-between his son's eyes. Blue smoke rose from the wound. Crimson blood oozed out the back of Bobby's head and to the floor as the blue smoke kept rising up and through the ceiling. A white flash shot from his son's eyes, blinding Jeremiah for a split second.

He dropped on his back and cried in a puddle of blood; his family dead beside him.

CHAPTER 3

Jeremiah Wash laid next to his family, unable to move for what felt like months to him. Although it was not really months, but three days had indeed passed; leaving his tears to be all but dried up after the first day. His face remained twisted in pain and as his body convulsed from long forgotten sobs. He looked over to where his son had fallen and then looked down to the rifle. His mind, cluttered with the lack of sleep and misery, immediately went to one single devastating thought.

Quickly, he sat upright; anger and pain behind his bloodshot eyes. He reached towards his Winchester and positioned himself up against the wall. The horrific scene before him caused him to breathe with severe anxiety, sadness, and shame. Not one single emotion could describe what was running through his mind; fear, self-hatred, sorrow, but above all, he felt calm for some unknown reason. He looked down at his rifle, the muzzle in his hand, barrel resting against the still open wound on his leg. Blood slowly seeped out. It had been somewhat healed for a time, only to be disturbed by his movements, ripping it open ever so slightly. Blood dripped from the butt end of his Winchester and onto the floor:

Drip…

Drip…

The puddle formed slowly, but with all of the thoughts dancing about his head, he barely noticed. The puddle didn't exist, his house didn't exist; only he and the rifle consumed the universe.

Drip…

Drip…

He could only focus on the borehole as an eye staring back into his slowly decaying mind. He contemplated, wondering what would happen next; would he see God? Would he see the Devil? If it were the latter; he knew he would be fighting, destroying the face of Lucifer himself while demanding answers to where the demon that did this may be. He would be relentless in his fight, no matter what trickery the Devil may play, he would pursue and punish until the location of the demon that made him kill his son was revealed. And then, once he knew where to find that lowly piece of shit, he would do everything in his power to make sure it never harmed anyone again. He would fight it until the rapture, yet he felt that had already come.

Drip…

He thought of God; of his eternal light. Would God be able to forgive the atrocity of murdering his first and only son? Jeremiah knew well of the story of Abraham and how God told him to sacrifice his son. However, there was no Angel of the Lord calling from Heaven, there was no altar constructed, no specific instructions; it was just a father killing his son. There was no lamb to take the place of Bobby's young soul.

There would be no redemption.

Drip...

The borehole called to him once more, whispering the only thing he wanted at this point in his life. The Devil? God? An angel? Demon? Is any entity watching over him, feeling his pain with him, sympathizing with his debate? Is there even anything out there; any controlling power? This was the first time in his life he questioned his faith, the first time in his life that he could not see a God watching over him. No Jesus, no Allah, no Devil, no Buddha; just a lonely grieving sinner.

Drip...

He quickly glanced up at the small window above his bed. The fog was still there, hanging over what he thought was the most beautiful land in existence. Would this breath of evil ever lift to let him see the land that he called home? Texas skies were always so beautiful, wide, almost never ending. Even when the storms rolled over the prairie there was a sense of beauty; every lightning strike, a drop of rain had its own harmony about it. Now there was nothing but that fog, smoky and hanging about. Nothing but pure evil to destroy his mind and his entire life. This was the end.

Drip...

The first time he laid eyes on his Jennifer he was only sixteen years old. She was in the church, helping her parents pass around small amounts of food in celebration for an expected child. Jennifer's mother was showing signs of pregnancy, but Jeremiah completely forgot about that; he only remembered Jennifer's hair tied up in a bun, her eyes reflecting beauty from her soul into his. He fell in love instantly.

drip...

He began courting her a short while later, and she fell in love without hesitation. They married a few days before his 20th birthday, vowing to love each other in the very same church where they first met.

drip...

He remembered when Bobby was first brought into the world. He was perfect; eyes twinkling up at his Daddy, his mother laying in the bed smiling through her exhaustion. The first time he saw Jennifer hold their child it was as if everything was going to be perfect; a beautiful family. He kept that memory as a painting that would never fade, hanging in his mind, as the happiest memory of his life.

drip…

The trigger was calling him, screaming out his sins one by one. The barrel was whispering everything he wanted to hear.

drip…

The bullet was ready to kiss him.

drip…

drip…

drip…

He slowly maneuvered the barrel up, placing it under his chin. The cold steel sent a chill down his spine; coursing through his nerves and into his legs and arms. He sat there frozen for a moment, before finding the courage to move his hand towards the trigger. That is when the loss of blood and lack of sleep finally took him over, and he fell off to his side as the room blurred around him.

drip…

He awoke, he hadn't known how long he'd been asleep, and looking out the window was no help as it appeared just the same as it had for the past couple of days. His Winchester's barrel was facing past his head and out the door. He studied it carefully; absorbing every scratch and grind, almost as if viewing every single imperfect stroke from when it was made. He contemplated the same thought, the idea of a bullet allowing him to greet whatever was on the other side. He thought of God, wondering if there was anything looking over him. The trigger was no longer speaking; it was just as lifeless as it had always been before all of this. And then, he saw his son and wife sprawled out before him.

Through fresh tears he picked up the rifle, laying it across his lap as he sat up against the wall once more. The pain in his leg had mostly subsided; the puddle of blood mostly dried to black on the floor. He looked at the wooden parts of the rifle; the stock and the forend. He lifted the rifle, holding it as he would if he were walking through his property searching for a coyote, or possibly an intruder. Not quite at the ready; but almost there. He felt the wood on his hand, pressed against his shoulder; his finger hovering ever so slightly above the trigger. He looked at his son once more.

Suddenly, and without knowing, he placed the rifle back on his lap and reached for his satchel in one single motion. He pulled out his knife and began carving into the forend of his rifle. Wood shavings slowly fell to crusted blood on the floor; the only sound in the room was the knife's blade meeting with the wood. He took care in his carving, making sure it wouldn't interfere with his grip on the rifle, that it wouldn't interfere with the way he held and aimed. With care, he carved in each individual letter.

B. He checked the craftsmanship of the lines and curves, feeling it with his fingertips. His eyes closed just for a quick moment.

O. He did his best to make sure that it was in line with the first letter carved. Only slightly off; he would be the only one who could notice. Still, he tried to correct it the best he could.

B. The knife was trembling in his hand, yet still able to make the marks in the varnished wood. He checked the letters; seeing how they appear against the darkened stained wood.

B. His vision slowly went blurry, just long enough to where the lower loop on the B was off by just enough. He fixed the line to where it connected to the bottom loop, unfortunately, it made it just marginally larger than the other letters by roughly three millimeters.

Y. All of the letters were finally carved in; it wasn't perfect, but it was close to him. His heart slightly fluttered with pain, but he knew it would only mean something to him. He held the rifle up, looking down the barrel as if ready to shoot. He wanted to see how it felt in his hand.

His eyes began to well up with tears as he ran his fingertips over the newly carved letters, brushing away the bits of shavings onto the floor. He saw that some fell into the large blood crusted area just below his leg. He checked his wound; seeing it had begun to heal while he was incapacitated. He saw the rivers of blood that once flowed down his calf had become the cracked color of red and white, hair piercing through the little islands forming on the delta of blood. At that moment, something came over him, and the tears dissipated from his eyes. He stood up, pain throbbing in his leg; he hobbled as he walked to the door. Before leaving he turned and looked at his wife and child, he knew what he had to do.

The dirt began to fill in the newly dug holes, dropping on his wife and child's face. There were no tears as he covered them up, no real emotion expressed on his face other than exhaustion. He shoveled on until their graves had become small mounds next to his house. At the end of each mound, he hammered in crudely made wooden crosses with their names carved into them. He limped around to see the crosses behind the mounds and fell to his knees. He reached into his pocket and pulled out a cigarette. With a trembling hand, he lit it, inhaling the smoke, and then blew it up to where a blue sky should be.

He retrieved his bible from his satchel, flipping through the pages until he found the verse he wanted and began to recite it aloud as he held a small cross that he hung around his neck;

> *"The Lord is my shepherd; I shall not want. He maketh me to lie down in green pastures: he leadeth me beside the still waters. He restoreth my soul: he leadeth me in the paths of righteousness for his name's sake. Yea, though I walk through the valley of the shadow of death, I will fear no evil: for thou art with me; thy rod and thy staff they comfort me."*

He closed the bible, putting it back into the satchel as he puffed slowly on the cigarette. He wondered if it was any good now that it seemed he and his family had been left behind during the rapture. But still, it gave him some sense of hope and calm, some normalcy in the chaotic world. The cigarette burned its sweet scent into the stagnant dead air as he continued to stare at those simple wooden crosses. This was not at all how he thought the funeral would be for his wife. He had always thought that when her time came, he would be smiling from heaven, waiting for her to enter those gates to embrace and hold for all of eternity. But now, it was just him, his rifle, a pistol, and a lit cigarette at the very end of its moment in time. He took one final drag before raising to his feet.

He re-entered his home for one final time to change his clothes and gather supplies. He filled his satchel with the remaining bit of tea leaves, some bread, and as much tobacco as he could hold before finding a fresh pair of pants and a shirt. He grabbed his long brown duster hanging from a hook by the front door as he exited and set off to the darkened horizon of fog.

CHAPTER 4

The terrain had changed from what he was used to. Somewhere, off in the distance, a bridge appeared; it seemed to raise up from the ground only to form an arch and return to the earth. He approached, still limping. He knew this had to have been the way to town, yet he wondered where this structure came from. As he got closer, he noticed the bridge was in disrepair; made of what appeared to be large light yellow stones. From each end, a long, flat, gray road seemed to stretch on for miles and off over the darkened horizon. He noticed some peculiar objects placed oddly on the bridge. Against his good senses, he walked up to investigate.

They seemed to be some sort of carriages with black wheels and bodies made of steel. He couldn't find any area for the horses to be attached to; so they seemed more like small trains with no tracks. One of them had *FORD* written in large block letters on the back. He inspected the doors and found a few of them were not jammed. Forging around inside of the small trains, he searched for food, water, and any other supplies he could. In one of them, he found a strange looking pack full of first aid supplies that he had never seen before, but decided they may come in handy. In another one, he found two half empty clear canteens of water. Yet another had the jackpot; a full bottle of whiskey sealed in a clear paper. He climbed onto the roof of one of the small trains to look out into the distance; nothing but desolate terrain and forgotten vehicles. He felt he was all that was left on this once beautiful planet.

He continued to scan the horizon for some time; the town should have been visible by now, even though the dense fog had drastically reduced visibility. Or maybe – possibly – this was where the town once stood. He could see nothing that looked familiar to him. There was no church, store, saloon, houses, brothel; it was all gone.

The sun, or where he thought the sun should be, had not changed position through his entire time in this Hell. He couldn't tell exactly where in the sky the sun may be, but it was the same brightness it had been the entire day. He was weary from his long trek and knew he needed to find himself an acceptable place to rest. He inspected the vehicles scattered on the bridge in order to find one that he could sleep in without being seen. He found one, blue in color, with a large area in the back; the door dropped down to reveal a small crawl space only about one and a half feet tall. He inspected the inside to make sure there was some way to open it again once he closed the small drop down door.

Unfortunately, although he could raise the top to an angle, he could not find a way to prevent the door from locking once it closed. He searched a while more, checking all of the vehicles for anything to jam the lock while keeping it closed.

He found some rope that he could tie around a small loop he had seen on the inside of the door, but he needed to re-inspect the inside to see if he could tie it off somewhere. But, it wouldn't do much to prevent it from locking. He went back and inspected his "bed" to figure out a way to prevent it from locking him in. He noticed on either side of the door, there were small metal brackets that seemed to hold the door upright. He figured if he could break off these brackets, he could just tie the rope off to hold it closed, and then just untie it to open it again.

He again began to check the other vehicles for anything to break the brackets free. In one of the vehicles, he found a long metallic object on an "L" shape and figured it would work well. He made his way back to the area he was going to sleep and began hammering away at the brackets. The bangs echoed off the gray road, but quickly dissipated, being swallowed up by the fog in the distance. He freed the brackets and tested his theory that it would prevent the door from staying closed; he was, fortunately, right. He hastily rigged up the inside with rope and settled himself inside. It was pitch black, cramped, but an acceptable temporary shelter. He placed a small cross that he carried at the entrance, took off his duster and folded it into a pillow, and slowly began his descent into dreams.

He awoke in the pitch-black shelter he had made, groggy and alone. He realized one critical flaw in his attempts to make a safe place to sleep; he had no way of looking out without opening the small door. He had no way of making sure no one was out there, no way of making sure the demons were kept at bay as he slept. He untied the rope; holding it as to make sure the door didn't lower for a moment as he made his way slowly to it. He slowly lowered the door to find that nothing had changed, not even the everlasting fog had dissipated. Seeing that the nothing new was in sight, he exited and began scanning the horizon once more.

Everything seemed to be the exact way it had been the day before, vast stretching grey road with the same strange vehicles on it. He figured he should stay here for another day or so to recuperate before venturing off once more into the abyss. He ate some of the bread he had brought with him and opened up the bottle of whiskey he found. Whiskey, to him, was the best medicine he could have; it was better than any medical equipment he had ever come across. It drowned out the thoughts of having to kill his own son, see his wife torn apart. It doused that flame that burned in his broken soul.

He had to first attend to the matter of finding a way to look outside of his shelter without having to open the door. It could be done by just simply putting a few bullets into it to make small peep-holes, but he decided against it as he didn't want to waste ammunition. He noticed that the bar that he used to break off the brackets of the door had an almost point at one end. He rammed it against the steel of the vehicle, but it only made a deep dent and scratched off some of the blue to revealing the bare metal underneath. He tried again, but unfortunately, the same result came of it. He decided to inspect the other vehicles once more in order to find something else in order to procure the wanted result.

He had already picked through the vehicles which doors were not jammed and knew if he was going to be able to find any new supplies he had to break into the others. He took the bar and broke one of the windows of the nearest vehicle. Instantly, he fell to his knees and covered his ears as the vehicle began to flash and wail, piercing the pristine silence with high pitched screeches. It echoed off into the distance, beeping and screaming as if in a pain of its own. He just stayed there, on his knees, until the noise subsided. When it finally did, he checked the horizon; to his relief nothing had changed. *Not doing that again* he thought to himself as he reached into the vehicle and began searching around. Lucky for him, it was the only vehicle he had to break into. In the back was a toolbox full of many useful items, a box that said it contained "200 fine rolled cigarettes" as well as food in boxes and in cans. He had to make two separate trips in order to bring it all back to his little site.

He looked at the horizon once more; still no change. He sat down, opened the bottle of whiskey once more and took a swig. He looked at the food he'd collected; some canned beans, some different soups, and 2 boxes that said *Granola bars* on it. He decided to open one of the boxes; inside he found an assortment of items wrapped in a metallic paper. He read each individual wrapper until he decided to try the one that was labeled as *chocolate chip*; it was delicious. He sat and enjoyed the food for a moment, and then lit himself a cigarette. He looked at the box of cigarettes he had; a picture of a camel in the desert, a pyramid in the background. *A box of cigarettes?* He thought to himself while smoking his hand rolled cigarette; *interesting.* He took another swig of whiskey before he decided it was time to figure out if any of the tools would make a sufficient hole in the shelter.

He popped open the toolbox, pulling every item out and laying it before him. A screwdriver and hammer would do just fine, unfortunately, there was no hammer. Still, he pushed a screwdriver against the side of the shelter and hit it with the metal rod he found earlier; success! Finally, he found a way to keep his shelter properly fortified while at the same time keeping him hidden and safe.

He sat on the blue swing-down door, staring off into the distance. *Nothing ever changes now*, he thought to himself through a puff of smoke. Taking several more swigs of whiskey, he knew his mind would grow fuzzy relatively soon; *Good*, he thought. As he lit another cigarette, the whiskey did indeed take over; his sight became slightly distorted, his coherence to the surroundings became lagged. He felt the forend of his rifle, pain swelled up from his fingertips and coursed into his spine. Shivers eventually made their way up to his neck; he gripped his rifle, and slowly began to pick it up. The barrel once again called to him, so he placed it under his chin. His finger slowly began to feel every scratch and nick along the trigger. His eyes closed, tears rushed down his face, he was ready. His finger, trembling, began to apply pressure to the trigger. Suddenly his eyes snapped open as he heard the screams and cries of someone in distress somewhere off in the distance.

Jeremiah looked off into the distance, trying to figure where the cries were coming from. The noise seemed to be coming from all directions.

BANG BANG BANG!

Shots, off somewhere in the distant fog, the cries dimmed out and almost disappeared completely. He could still hear a faint cry and a man yelling in a language he had never heard before.

Something had happened, and someone possibly needs help. He pushed the whiskey from his mind, for just a moment, only long enough to pinpoint on the hushed cries of pain and terror. As soon as he knew which direction to head off in, he began a sprint; swaying side to side drunkenly, hand gripping his small .22 caliber pistol. The landscape blurred and wobbled as his feet contacted the hard ground.

His shelter had disappeared from sight; the crying grew slightly louder with every step he took. His breath amplified in his ears as he ran; he had to make sure he could do something. Slowly two small shadows appeared off in the distance, and he knew that this had to be where the crying was coming from. He slowed his pace to a brisk walk, his head on a swivel, hand still glued to his pistol.

It was two children, huddled together, crying. As soon as they saw him approaching, they ducked behind a pile of clothes that was in front of them. He stopped dead in his tracks; they were hiding behind a still bleeding body of a man. He didn't know what to do, he just stood there, looking at the body and back to the little eyes peering at him behind it. He took his hand off of his pistol and again began to slowly approach.

"Hey there, you two alright?" He said calmly, holding his hands open and in front of him, doing his best to appear non-threatening. He could see them duck behind the body, laying almost flat, hiding from him. "I'm not here ta hurt ya'," he came closer to the point where they could no longer hide, he could see their backs huddled and crying.

"Don't hurt us!" One of them said softly through tears, clenching an opal necklace tight as if it were a crucifix.

"I would never," He said, kneeling down, "Are you alright? Are ya' hurt?"

"Our daddy!" The other said, "We were just on our way home, they didn't have to…"

"Shhhh! Shhh, it's alright" Jeremiah put his hand on the crying child's back. He could tell that they were young; the one he was comforting could only be about five, the other maybe nine. He coerced them away from their father; three bullet holes in his lifeless body. He wanted to freeze, but he knew he had to do something. "Where did they go?" He asked.

"W-w-who?" The older one said, shaking.

"The ones who did this," he asked as the older child hugged the younger one tight against her chest, burying the child's face so she could cry. She then pointed in the direction that Jeremiah had been traveling when he found the two. "Wait here, I'll be back for ya'." The child nodded as he set off quickly in the direction he was pointed in.

He wandered, checking the ground for tracks of any kind. Every now and then he found some strange scratches in the dried dirt. He continued, wondering where those responsible may have vanished off to. And just then, he heard something. He stopped, pushing the whiskey away from his mind, just long enough to hear the laughing of some men in the direction he was walking. He doubled his pace; silent, but quick, forward on. Four figures appeared in the fog, black silhouettes against the grey skyline. One of them appeared to be walking slightly hunched over, dragging something behind them. He was so close; he could almost hear their light footsteps.

He slowed ever so slightly, just enough to be completely silent in his pursuit. Unfortunately, the whiskey betrayed him as he stumbled over his own feet, catching himself just barely. A voice called from one of the figures, and instantly he was surrounded by them. They had large eyes, circular noses connecting to a trunk that coiled onto their backs; demons in Jeremiahs eyes. He pulled his pistol and was instantly greeted by the barrels of rifles against him. "C'wboy, what business you have?" A thick accent, muffled and unrecognizable to Jeremiah came from one of the faces.

"Seems ta me" he replied, hand still gripping his pistol "y'all got somethin' that don't belong to ya'. Also, not too happy with ya' killin' two little girl's daddy."

Laughter erupted from expressionless faces, and then Jeremiah felt a sharp pain in the back of his head; everything went dark for just a split second. He reached up to feel the back of his head, warm and wet with blood. He rose to his feet quickly, drawing his pistol; trying to steady his aim. Their laughter subsided for just a quick moment as they took aim, but then lowered their weapons and erupted in laughter once more.

"C'wboy, stupid bitch!" the same one called through laughter, "drunk! Don't know not to drink on the road, in the Grey!"

"Now," Jeremiah said through their laughter, "I may've been drinkin', but I still got a damn good shot." He turned, placing a bullet through one of the large eyes of the demon behind him. Before the other three could react, he spun around and put second bullet through the mouth of another. As the bullet left his pistol, he began to fall backwards; he lost his balance due to the mix of alcohol and hit to the back of his head. This time, falling had been lucky for Jeremiah, as bullets excited the rifles of the two remaining standing demons; one bullet from each.

As soon as Jeremiah hit the ground he pulled the trigger, hitting one of the demons in the neck. Blood spurted out with each heartbeat as the demon fell down to the ground; dropping his rifle and gripping his wound. The final demon was pulling back the bolt to reload, but it was not fast enough; Jeremiah shot up from the ground, pulling out his knife. He plunged his knife into the demon's gut, coming face to face as their foreheads touched. Inside of the large eyes, he saw the eyes of a man, fear engulfing them until the symphony of death consumed him.

Jeremiah drug a small sleigh that was covered by a blanket; two young girls following behind him. A small wooden cross disappeared in the distance as Jeremiah's shelter came into view. They walked at a steady pace until they reached the safety of that small blue vehicle.

"Y-you" the oldest child began, nervously playing with her necklace, "you live in a, in a, a pickup truck?"

Jeremiah looked down at the child, some confusion in his eyes, "I suppose so." He said, putting the sleigh just under the pickup truck at the door. "Any pillows or blankets in here?" He asked, gesturing to the sleigh as he lit a cigarette.

"Some." The oldest replied, looking over to the pickup truck and back to the sleigh.

"Your sister alright? She ain't said much. I mean, I know ya' been through a lot." He paused, took a drag from his cigarette. He looked at the older child, studying her face for a moment. "Never mind. Why don't y'all get some sleep." He nodded his head to the door he'd been using for his shelter.

"But, what if something happens? The Grey is s-so weird."

"Don't you worry none; I'll keep a lookout. Try n' rest a bit."

The children climbed into the back of the pickup truck, pulling in some blankets with them. As they closed the door, the youngest looked straight into Jeremiah's eyes, moving her lips ever so slightly as if saying something silently to herself. The door closed, and Jeremiah felt alone again, except he had another purpose now; get the children to their mother. Suddenly his eyelids felt heavy; he took a swig of whiskey and went to take another drag of his cigarette. Before it reached his lips he fell off to his side, falling asleep instantly.

Jeremiah was standing in a veil of nothingness. Nothing, no one; just him and his rifle. He inhaled, taking in the cool air. He turned left and right, trying to find some sign of where he was, yet nothing came into view.

"You're new to the Grey," a child's voice said from behind him, "aren't you?"

Jeremiah quickly turned around, his rifle at the position to fire; and there staring into his eyes was the youngest child he had just saved. He breathed in deep, lowered his rifle, then kneeled down to get at eye level with the little girl. "What do ya' mean?"

"The Grey." The child replied, looking deeply into Jeremiah's eyes, "It's what we all call this. The fog that rolled in, the strange

happenings; it's all because of the Grey."

"I see," He looked over his shoulder; nothing.

"Yes. I was born in it; my mommy and daddy had me about 2 years after they fell through. My sister isn't from it though, but she may as well be if you think about how almost her whole life has been in the Grey. Mommy tells me stories about what it was like before." She paused, looking at his rifle, studying his attire "You're a cowboy!" Excitement raised in her voice as she clasped her hands together.

Jeremiah chuckled, "Well, not exactly; I'm a rancher. But, I do like 'cowboy', maybe I should just say that's what I am."

"You know this is a dream, right? I'm sorry, but I just had to see your mind; I was afraid of you."

"Afraid of me?"

"Yes... it's hard to tell who to trust. But I like you; you're a good man!" She hugged him. Jeremiah felt the warmth consume him as her little arms embraced him. "You were just making sure we were ok, thank you so much."

Jeremiah felt her tears wetting his shirt as she buried her face into his shoulder and began to cry. He hushed her, brushing her hair gently and calmly, trying to figure out the right words to say in order to comfort her.

"Yup," she said through tears of relief, "You're a good man; thank you so much."

"I'll make sure you make it home; don't you worry none; not for a second."

"I know, thank you, cowboy." She kissed him on the cheek and then vanished into the white nothingness. He felt his shoulder that she had cried on; still damp and warm. A great sigh exited his lungs as he closed his eyes, praying for the world to go back to how it was before all that had happened.

Jeremiah awoke, cold and outside of the shelter where the two children had been sleeping. The dream lingered in his head; *what did it mean?* He looked down at the almost empty whiskey bottle, he contemplated finishing it but decided he had to be on his guard to get the children back home. He adjusted his hat, lit a cigarette, and checked his pistol. He knew he'd need to get some more .22 ammunition as soon as he could and hoped that maybe wherever these children were from would have a store of some kind. He remembered the food was in the pickup with the kids; he was feeling a little hungry but knew he should let them sleep a while more.

He stood up and scanned the horizon once more, trying to find any signs of life, but the desolate scenery offered none as usual. His head throbbed with pain from every heartbeat. Maybe now would be a good time to address the wound before heading out. He opened his satchel; pulling out some of the medical supplies he had acquired from one of the strange vehicles. He studied them in an attempt to figure out what would be best suited for a head wound. One bottle, labeled *hydrogen peroxide* said it could be used to prevent infection. He opened it, pouring it carefully over the back of his head; it stung and fizzed, making him wince slightly. He let the stinging subside before taking some bandages to complete patching himself up.

I hope they know where to go, he thought to himself again. He sat down and waited to wake them, cleaning his pistol and rifle in the silent Hell that surrounded him.

CHAPTER 5

The oldest child walked alongside the sled that held supplies, her little sister riding on top of it. Before they set off, Jeremiah had inspected their belongings as they watched, and was able to find a crude hand-drawn map. None of the landmarks looked familiar to Jeremiah, except a small object that appeared to be the bridge he had spent the last few days on. Using that as a reference, they set off in the direction that seemed to be towards the children's home. They stopped from time to time to have a bite, water; and in Jeremiah's case, a smoke.

As they walked, Jeremiah would turn back randomly, making sure that the two girls were still in tow. If the oldest one started to trail off behind him, he would slow down, just a little, so she felt like she was keeping up on her own. He wanted her to feel as in control of the situation as he possibly could. Part of him kept forgetting their details, and the truth is he wanted to forget. For him, knowing their features would make him get attached, and with everything he's experienced in the Grey, he told himself he had to forget. If he remembered the youngest one's blue eyes, the oldest one's black hair, it would be harder on him if something happened to them. However, he knew this wouldn't help at all. All he knew is he had to protect them.

Whenever he could, he would check the map; trying to see if that tree they passed was on it, or the small house with no door. Sometimes it was, other times it wasn't, and when it wasn't he began to question the direction they were traveling. But still he knew he had to continue on; he had to make sure the kids were brought home safely. Hours of travel, and still no sign of a town or any recent human activity.

He decided they could pause at the next landmark; what looked like a church with a tall tree in the front of it. In order to get the pace up, he called out to the oldest one, "Hey you! Why don't ya' come on up here?"

The older child looked over to her little sister; searching for some sort of assurance that it would be alright for her to walk ahead. The little one simply smiled at her older sister, and then looked up at Jeremiah. The older one hurried her pace and eventually caught up with Jeremiah as he walked.

"So, ya' think you'll be alright if we stop at the next landmark?" Jeremiah asked, "We've been traveling for a good while, an' I'm sure your feet could use a rest; Lord knows mine could" Jeremiah chuckled for a second, then looked down at the child; she seemed to pay him no mind. "You alright there, little one?"

"Sasha." She said without looking up.

"What?"

"My name is Sasha." She said, her hand was again playing with the opal hanging from her neck. "You don't have to keep calling me *little one*, or *kid*. I'm *Sasha*."

Jeremiah could hear the pain in her voice; her mind was wandering to her father, a lonely grave that wasn't even marked on any map for anyone to find. He was a memory, lonesome and lost in the minds of two children. Only they would know his dying breath; that exhale and twinkle escaping the pupils of his eyes. He tried to figure out a way to comfort her, but his mind instantly wandered to a simple name; *Sasha*. He tossed her name around a few times in his head. Now she has a name; at least to him, she had just acquired the name, a name she has had her whole life. But now she has entrusted him with her name.

"Well, Sasha," He began, glancing down at her, "You and your sister have been..."

"Her name is Ma-Ma-*Marie*" Sasha cut him off, still refusing to make eye contact.

And now, he had two names; two names that forced their way into his mind. Two names, he had not anticipated feeling more of a need to protect those two; but with names, he only could protect them more. Something inside of him seemed to light on fire; *I should be protecting my boy*, he thought. Unfortunately, he could not hide the pain on his face very well.

Sasha glanced up at just the right moment, "I-I'm sorry..." She looked down and away towards her small feet.

Jeremiah snapped back to reality; "No, no, you're fine; just thinkin' 'bout the past." He took one hand and patted her on the shoulder. She looked up to see him forcing a smile at her. "Just, ya' know, had one of those thoughts... We all have 'em!" He smiled bigger and turned his head to face forward. Somehow he had to regain his composure, not for his sake, but for the sake of Sasha and Marie.

A building with a tree in front of it began to seemingly materialize out of the fog. He slowed their approach, trying to study the entire area and make sure it was completely safe before they arrived. Something caught his eye in the church; as if a figure was anticipating their arrival in the shadow of the holy structure. He made sure not to make the figure known to the children as they finally reached the outside of the church.

The cross that sat atop seemed to be the only thing that remained untouched by the Grey; as it was pristine and almost new, copper that still reflected what little light shown onto it. The structure itself, although solid, seemed to have been through many storms that never were able to destroy it. He put the sled at the base of the tree and told the girls to wait with it so he could inspect the church.

"Just gotta make sure it's safe." He said, kneeling to reach eye-level with the Sasha and Marie, "Wouldn't want to try to sleep in somethin' if it ain't safe." With that, he patted Sasha on the shoulder and ruffled Marie's hair before turning towards the structure and approached it slowly, methodically.

He scanned every inch of the outside of the structure, absorbing all that he saw, searching for the shadow in the windows. Unfortunately, the windows only revealed their age and ill-maintenance; hairline cracks and holes etched throughout every window on the structure. The steps leading up to the large double-doors seemed to almost decay under his feet as he climbed them carefully. His hand instinctually gripped his pistol as he pushed the doors open. They whined and creaked, opening just enough for him to slip inside. He was hit with a rush of warm stagnant air, cutting into his nostrils and stealing his breath for a moment.

Looking inside, he saw the house of God in complete disorder and disarray; the pews were scattered across the floor, bibles strewn about. Suddenly he noticed a hunched figure at the front of the church, kneeling as if in prayer near the pulpit. Brown robes barely gave away his kneeling position, a hood covering his head. Jeremiah got a slight tingle at the back of his neck, making its way to every extremity. The figure slowly rose to its feet; "Come in, child." It said without lifting its head from its slight bow. It walked over the large cross, ornately hung behind the preacher's podium. It raised a hand, touching Jesus' feet.

Jeremiah never took his hand from his pistol as walked through the church, trying to scan the entire area; looking for any other figures cloaked in the shadows. "Please," The figure said again, hand still on Jesus' foot, "The winds will be coming soon enough, I'd prefer the doors be secured. Call your little ones in as well, we wouldn't want them to fall to the tragic storm." The figure turned to face Jeremiah, yet its face remained shrouded in darkness, "Now, now, now, there is no need for a weapon, child." Suddenly, Jeremiah's pistol was no longer in his holster; instead, it was being held, non-threateningly, by the hooded figure. It placed the pistol on the ground beneath Jesus' feet. "No violence here, not in his house."

"Sorry, sir, but I can't bring them inside. No offense to ya', but I don't know ya'; don't know your intentions here." Jeremiah began to step backwards to the door, never letting his eyes leave the hooded figure.

"Now, now. I'm but a Friar in a strange land; cursed by a strange happening of the Devil. I find my strength in the Lord." He made a cross with his right hand, "I am nothing but a servant, as you are, Jeremiah Washington."

Jeremiah froze dead in his tracks; goosebumps of fear ran from his spine to his fingertips. He gripped his holster with one hand, while slowly reaching for his rifle that was slung on his back; trying to make his movements as clean and slow as possible.

"Child, again, I am but a humble friar; I mean you no harm at all. However, I must insist you keep your weapons from your hands, as I wish no blood to be shed in *his* house."

"Then why is your face hidden?" Jeremiah snapped under his breath.

The figure sighed, "Because my face has been taken from me." It slowly lowered its hood to expose a faceless head; no eyes or nose, no mouth, just skin with cracks and holes like the windows of the church. "Unfortunate, but that is what happens when you stand against the new Gods; or at least those that are unforgiving. Now, please," He turned from Jeremiah, pulling his hood back up, "Bring the children in; the storm will be here at any moment, and I cannot protect them while they are outside."

Before Jeremiah could respond, a loud crack of thunder entered into the church and echoed along the walls. Suddenly, rain and wind began to pummel the old structure. Jeremiah turned to run outside, only to be greeted by Marie running in through the door, followed by Sasha huffing as she pulled the sled inside. "S-s-sorry, but it began t-to rain, and the w-wind," Sasha said, "is it safe?"

Jeremiah quickly drew his rifle, turning in one motion to the hooded figure; but he was nowhere to be seen.

"What are you doing?" Sasha asked, her voice quaking with nervous fear.

Jeremiah was at a loss; the figure was gone; his pistol had appeared back in his holster. He tried to figure out the situation as quickly as possible, but his mind instantly went to protecting the two children.

He walked over to the door, as he pulled it open, it flung out with the force of the wind. He struggled to close it as the rain pelted into his face. Once he secured the door, he quickly scanned the room once more; nothing, just the random pews, and bibles strewn about. Slinging his rifle across his back, he began to pull some of the pews together to make a bed for the girls to sleep on, all the while trying to pay attention to what he was moving and what could be hiding under or around it. Nothing seemed to be out of place or dangerous, he slowly began to get comfortable, yet still, he kept his guard up.

The storm seemed to rage on, getting worse while Sasha and Marie slept soundly on the bed Jeremiah had made out of the pews for them. They looked content, lost in dreams; hopefully good ones. Jeremiah was tired, yet he kept alert and focused in case the hooded figure was to return. He read his bible, silently to himself, looking up after every sentence.

"Good book to be reading," the hooded figure whispered quietly, appearing next to Jeremiah out of thin air. Jeremiah jumped to his feet, startled by the figure, "Child, you must quiet yourself, the young ones have wandered off to sleep; we mustn't wake them." It patted the floor where Jeremiah was sitting, beckoning him to sit back down. Jeremiah refused, and instead he sat in a pew that was facing the figure and the girls.

"What the Hell are you?" He asked the figure, hand steady on his pistol.

"Please! Watch your language!" The figure again made a cross with its right hand. "We are in his house!"

"Answer my question!" Jeremiah snapped, ready to draw his pistol.

"I am a man, much like yourself. However, I have been here, in this once glorious Church, for more than thirty years. This is where I was born, long after the Grey consumed the land. This is all I ever knew. I praise the one true God, much like yourself, but this world is a strange one."

Jeremiah slightly eased off of his pistol; something about what he was saying made him think about the Grey. He knew the girls had been in it for some time, but over *thirty years*? He still wasn't completely comfortable with the faceless stranger, but he could somehow tell he meant no harm to the girls; still, his hand rested on the grip. "What was it you said earlier; about the *new Gods*?"

"I know, you haven't been in the Grey for long enough to understand, and I'm sorry for anything that may confuse you in my story. But I know I should begin before time awakens the young ones." He looked over his shoulder to the girls, before turning back to Jeremiah.

"I was born in this Church, to a mother that could not survive the trauma of having a child. She died alongside the other patrons, as the priest said a quiet prayer in her memory. From then on I remained within these walls, giving my life to the Lord." He made another cross with his hand, "I did my duty for the Church, doing my best to bring more patrons into the sermon; praying for us to lift this veil that inflicted the earth. Eventually, we became one of the most used churches – to our knowledge – in the Grey.

"About ten or so years ago, a man appeared at the steps, draped from head to toe in green and gray cloth. He stood quietly and diligently for some time before I approached him. I asked him if he needed any help or possibly prayer for whatever situation disturbed him. He looked at me, scars from the bottom of his eyes stretched down to his chin; fabric stitches holding his face together. He held out one hand, open palm to my head. I fell down in sheer pain as his voice entered my mind.

"*We are not pleased*, it said, *the only immortal God is not yours. Where is your precious God in the Mist? Friar… Friar… you dare take worshipers of the Goddess Whisper? She shall take your faith away. We shall have a new home for her child to feast and play, within these unholy walls.*

"Excruciating pain coursed from my eyes, down to my chin. I shut them to the sound of thunder, and then he was gone. I went inside only to hear the screams of horror from our congregation as their eyes fixed to mine. A storm just raged outside, as if God were angry with the Church and I. From then on, I have been alone in this church. Every day, the storm strikes, intense; trying to destroy the house of Christ. Whisper is angry with our Lord, and I do my best to make sure that our Lords house never falls." Lightning struck outside, illuminating the room as the wind continued to pummel the sides of the church.

Jeremiah tried to contemplate the story he had just heard, figuring out what he meant by another God. This Friar had been serving the Lord alone for some time, in a church that never seemed to yield to the storm that punished it every night. "I'm sorry, Friar," Jeremiah said quietly, looking to the cracked skin that was once a man's face. "Is that how you were able to take my pistol so quick, knew my name?"

36

"No, child, that was simply my gift from when I was born. I know not how I ascertained such a gift. The original priest of this church said that from time to time angels find those born in the Grey, gifting them with powers from the Lord."

"A gift? From angels in the Grey? I'm sorry, friar, but that doesn't make a lick of sense." Jeremiah rubbed his temples, then his eyes; exhaustion slowly taking his mind over. He had no meetings with angels, no sign of God.

"The children, born out in this mist, something happens to them if the angels wish them to have it. When I was born, I could reach into the minds of others, feel their thoughts. I also am able to manipulate solid objects; myself included. I hid it for my entire life, not wanting to be an abomination of the Lord, for even if it were his gift, it felt unholy to me. I was also afraid that others would see the Devil in my powers, banish me from the Church to starve in the Grey alone.

"However, this is not the work of any fallen angel, it is but the work of the ones wandering within the rolling fog. This fog seems to have its own power as well. It seems to be its own God."

"I see." Jeremiah stood up. "Can I ask a favor of you, Friar?"

"Anything, Child."

"Could you please not reveal yourself to the girls? I'm trying to get 'em home, and I don't want 'em to be spooked by nothin', especially after what they've seen."

"Ah, yes, their poor father. I respect that, and I will stay out of sight, but do not leave as this storm rages." The Friar stood up and made his way to a shadowed corner of the room. "Now, find yourself some sleep, Jeremiah. I shall say a prayer for the peace needed for their father."

"Thank you, Friar."

The friar stood and began to walk away through the chaotic pews. Jeremiah made himself comfortable in a pew closest to the girls, his head resting against the hard stained wood.

Jeremiah awoke, feeling much more rested than he had in the past few days; the girls were still sound asleep in the bed that he had made them the night before. The claps of thunder had almost completely subsided, yet the patter of rain continued on as it had when he had first fallen asleep. He checked his effects, making sure everything was in order before he got up and began walking about the church. Eventually, he found himself, kneeling at Jesus' feet, looking up at his savior on a cross of wood, silver, and gold.

He remained there for a moment, saying a prayer in his head; a prayer for everything to be alright, for it all to go back to some sense of normalcy. He prayed that he would find the strength to get Marie and Sasha home safe, without incident, without drinking himself into oblivion. It was hard to concentrate on anything other than getting those girls home and drinking to forget about his past. Why did he have to be put in the situation where it seemed there were no good ending for him? He had his faith, his cigarettes, his gun, and whiskey; that was all Jeremiah felt he was, odds and ends of a typical hunting trip.

The patter of rain dissipated completely during the time he spent kneeling there. He looked out of one of the damaged windows to see the puddles fresh on the ground slowly soaking the dirt to mud. He knew it was time to get the girls up and get ready to continue on. He softly stepped over to the sleeping girls; they were so peaceful curled up under a torn old blanket. He shook Sasha lightly on the shoulder to wake her. She looked up at him with her bright glistening eyes; red filled the whites as she rubbed the sleep away. There was a slight twinkle in her eye; the type of twinkle you only see when someone smiles with hope, knowing they are safe. His heart lifted for a brief moment with the thought that even for a split second he made her feel safe. She rolled over and woke her sister, it took a short while, but eventually Marie did stir and opened her blue eyes. Unfortunately for Jeremiah, as soon as she woke up, he realized that her eyes were almost the same color blue as his beloved wife and son; and his heart sank down into the depths of his soul to hide away.

He turned away and picked up his items as the girls gathered their belongings onto the sled. Jeremiah opened the door, scanning quickly to make sure nothing or no one was waiting for them to come out of the church; nothing suspicious caught his eye. He whistled over to the girls, beckoning them to get a move on, and they hastily made their way towards him. Sasha exited the doors first, cautiously, and then waving to her sister to come out. Marie stepped out, looking up at Jeremiah, smiling at him as she passed. Jeremiah caught a pain in his throat, forcing it back down to his stomach. He looked to the shadows in the church to see the Friar emerge from one of them; the hood bowed as his right hand made a cross in the air, and then he retreated back into the shadows. Jeremiah exited, being sure to secure the door behind them; he took hold of the sled and continued on.

CHAPTER 6

Something about the horizon changed drastically; where the sky had been in what felt like a constant gray twilight, it had suddenly become darker. Jeremiah halted, staring at the odd sight before him. Sasha walked up beside him, looking out to see what had stopped their progress. He looked down at her, and placed his hand on her shoulder; she looked up, puzzled. "Why did we stop?" She asked.

"Well, looks like somethin' in the sky changed."

She looked out to the horizon; seeing the darkness. "It's the Grey." She said, "Some places have light all the time, some have twilight, some dark, and other places have a cycle. At least, that's what dad told me."

"You sure know a good bit 'bout this whole Grey, don't ya?" Jeremiah snickered, and ruffled her hair. He noticed her smile, then he saw her hand move up to play with her necklace again. He looked ahead, eyes on the horizon, "That's somethin' precious, ain't it?"

"Huh?" she looked up, puzzled.

"That necklace," he gestured at the opal in her fingers, "Seems like you're always fiddlin' with it in some way."

"Yea, it is." She looked up, her deep brown eyes peering at him, "Mom gave it to me before we set off with Dad. She said it will protect me, help me find my way back home to her no matter what." She paused, tears slowly began to infiltrate her eyes. "That's where we were going, after my sister's surgery. Dad also wanted to see if there was a better town to live in. Mom doesn't feel safe there, and dad wanted to make sure she felt safe. We c-couldn't find a place," her voice began to crack and waver, "And, w-w-we turned to go b-back... t-that's when dad di..." her voice trailed off to a light crackle.

Jeremiah dropped to a knee, hugged her, feeling her tears slowly seep into his shirt. He shushed her as he rubbed her head. He leaned his head in, resting it against her hair, trying his best to help ease her mind. She could cry, she could cry all of her tears, he wasn't trying to stop that.

"Th-thank you, so m-much. Thank you, th-thank you... you're a, a hero..." she sobbed for a moment longer as Jeremiah closed his eyes, wishing she hadn't said that.

He may have saved her, but she didn't know his past; she hadn't seen him take the life of his own son. Was it *really* his son, though; could he say that because the body was there, the mind possibly wasn't? No, no, he had to shake the thought from his head. He had promised himself to get Sasha and Marie home safely, and that is exactly what he was going to do. He gave Sasha a quick squeeze. "Don't worry," he said, "let's get you and your sister home, huh? I'm sure your Ma' would love to see ya'; and soon."

Sasha wiped her tears from her eyes and looked up at Jeremiah. He caught her eyes and gave her a quick smile. She pushed herself up onto the ball of her feet, just high enough to where she could give him a quick gentle kiss on the cheek before falling back to her heels. She hurried back to the sled and hugged her sister. He looked back at their brief yet warm embrace. It was something he enjoyed; two children, sisters, who care about each other that much. He turned back to the direction they were traveling, and slowly began to put one foot in front of the other towards the distant home of the girls.

The darkened sky made it slightly harder to navigate; he made sure to keep a steady and safe pace, stopping from time to time just to make sure they could catch their bearings. The girls stayed close behind him; Marie was walking almost immediately behind Jeremiah; Sasha was keeping a watchful eye on the rear as best she could. The Grey was eerier with a darkened sky, the fog swirling around seemingly illuminated by its own accord; still, it was hard to make out anything more than five or so yards in any direction.

Marie was silently humming to herself, a tune that Jeremiah had never really heard, but he enjoyed its upbeat melody. He glanced back for a moment, just to make sure everything was in order. The sled was about a yard behind him, same as always, Sasha caught Jeremiah's short glance and so she smiled at him. He returned the smile and turned to face ahead once more.

He slowed down, almost to a stop; something was rustling in the mist somewhere around them. He pulled his rifle at the ready and brought them to a complete stop; he got down on a knee and scanned the horizon down the barrel of his rifle. Sasha grabbed Marie and huddled near Jeremiah; she attempted to make them seem as small as possible, just in case something were to happen. Although the sounds seemed to be close by, the constant mist concealed its source from them, but Jeremiah knew something had to be there.

Jeremiah tried to get Sasha's attention in order to give her the rope that he was using to pull the sled. He needed to keep both of his hands free in order to make sure he could take a shot if need be. She took it without letting go of her sister; he could tell that she was terrified by what was happening. Jeremiah gestured for them to follow him as he cautiously continued forward; step by step, heel to toe. Slow and quiet. The rustling continued, yet it never seemed to get any closer, nor any further away. He tried to pinpoint it, but to no avail. *Where is that rustling* he thought to himself.

Without fading, the rustling ceased. Jeremiah stopped moving forward; something was different, odd; the scent in the air even went from stale to the clean crispness of after a long rain. He turned, the girls were frozen in their tracks as if time had stopped. Sasha's hair was slightly askew from stepping; her eyes half open, frozen in a blink.

He tapped her on the shoulder yet gained no response. Everything was frozen completely; everything except for Jeremiah. He tried to make sense of it, looking around the two girls-turned-statues. He sniffed the air, aside from it no longer being stale and the new smell of rain, everything seemed as normal as possible, by Grey standards at least. He tried to figure out what had happened; why was he the only one that could move? He wondered if the girls could at least hear him, maybe see, but he had no way of knowing. From their direction of travel, Jeremiah heard footsteps lightly pressing against the soil as a tall, slender woman emerged from the fog.

Before Jeremiah stood a woman, wrapped in jade silk, nothing more. Her hair was an ice blue and clean, wavy at the ends. Her eyes were of a piercing violet, a long scar leading from the bottom of each down to her chin. Her lips velvet and outlined with a deep, blood red. She had a sense about her; something holy, yet unclean. Jeremiah didn't know how to react, but he stepped in between her and the children, his rifle fixed to her head; right in between her upper lip and the bottom of her nose.

"Now, now," she said, quietly, "You are not of the Grey, Jeremiah."

Jeremiah recoiled; keeping his sight fixed on the tall woman, sweat began to glisten on his brow. "A child born in the Grey, I assume. What damn angel visited you to give ya' some gift," He said, never letting his guard down.

"No, no," she said again, sweetly, quietly, "I am a God. I am a new God. I am an old God." Her lips curled up, almost in a menacing way covered in the sweetness of molasses.

"There's only one God, and I'm sure as shit you ain't him."

"Jeremiah, that is not how this works, not in the Grey. I am a God, a Goddess, a strong and simple Goddess." Her voice never rose from its sweet hushed tone, "I am who watches, I am who waits. I am the one who leads my child to feed on the unholy, leads my followers. I am the one who-"

"Save it," He shouted, cutting off her speech. He had the girls almost pressing against his back, attempting to protect them from the menacing figure. He wished he could have them turn and run; they had seen too much death for this point in their life, he wanted to save them from that. He felt helpless, but not hopeless.

"Save it?" she queried, voice still as calm as it had ever been, "I am Whisper, and I mean you no harm. Jeremiah, I only wish for you to join me, for you to *help* me."

Jeremiah thought back to the Friar; cursed by Whisper in the church that everyone had forgotten. He thought of how he had lost his face, but not his sight nor voice, and how his little church had to be pounded every night by the same storm. "I know of ya', and I ain't havin' none of it! You need to back away, right now, or else…"

"No!" the same calm voice left her perfect ruby lips, "I'm not here to harm you; you are just simply in my way. You have something that I want; more someone." Her eyes peered over to Marie then back to Jeremiah.

"Not happening." His finger was almost ready to squeeze the trigger, waiting for her to make the wrong move. "These girls are getting home; you're not stopping that. So, get outa the way, or I'll take ya' out."

"But I saved you! I allowed you to survive the frightful wrath of my child. You should have the decency, just one of them; the other will be safe and sound with the mother. I can even make sure no one remembers her. After all, she is only a child; not even your own…"

Jeremiah flinched slightly but kept his rifle aimed. Blood pumped through his body, he could hear it course into his head as it swirled around his brain. Sweat began to drip; cold. The sight of his rifle slowly moved, perfectly reflecting the barrel from her right eye. "Watch your tongue!" He shouted, slowly lowering the rifle from back to his original target, "Or I'll take it out of this world with a led bullet."

"Stop, you fool." She raised her hand; Jeremiah began to tremble uncontrollably. "I just am here for the child. I had to stop time, to make sure she was safe. Give her to me, I'll give you safe passage, but then I will come for you once the other is home so we may discuss the matters at hand. I promise the other one won't remember her; you won't remember her. It will be as if she never existed. You'll be safe, I promise." She stepped forward.

Jeremiah, quickly, lowered his rifle and shot Whisper in the left shin. She stumbled backward; liquid as clear as water spouted from her open wound. Her eyes turned from violet to deep red. She did not appear in pain, only anger came from her face. "I said; back away." He called as she stopped from her slight stagger; piercing her gaze through Jeremiah as if she were looking to the children he protected. His rifle raised once more to her head, "I will put you in the ground."

"You're an insolent fool! I offered you safe passage; one of the children to be home with her loving mother. I offered you all you could really need at this moment, yet you refuse. You are but a simple mortal, why are they so important to you?" Her eyes never moved.

A crack of thunder called out above them. It called for rain that never came in their standoff.

"Why are they so important to you? Why do you want them?"

"No, just one of them… and you," She looked down the barrel of his rifle, "Very well then, Jeremiah Washington, I see how you want it. I could have given you everything back; your life would have been yours again." She turned and began to walk away. As she became nothing more than a shadow she called behind her; "You could have taken her home…" She disappeared into the mist.

Jeremiah could hear the breath of the girls begin once more as the strange spell that was cast on the land lifted. He turned around, looking at Marie and Sasha, making sure they were still there; still safe. To his relief, nothing about them had changed; still young and afraid, but safe. "What," Sasha began, "What is it?"

"I blinked and… and you were closer, is everything ok?" Marie asked, terror filling her voice.

"No, don't worry; everything is gonna to be alright. C'mon, we should probably get a move on if we're to get ya' home." He forced a smile, doing his best to look like everything was as it should be. His deception worked, as the two appeared to come to an ease. He heard the rustling again, but it seemed to be slowing in frequency.

Suddenly he saw something out of the corner of his eye; a shadow in the mist. Massive, crouching, ready to take out its prey. A snarl could be heard. Jeremiah's blood ran cold as he readied his rifle once more. Before he could bring the barrel up to take aim, a wolf-like creature the size of a horse pounced towards the children. Six legs; the front two extended out as if it were a jaguar taking out a helpless animal. It's mouth open, showing sharp teeth, reflecting what little light came through the mist, glinting off the blackened points. Just as his rifle was at the ready the creatures mouth attached to Sasha.

Jeremiah fired his Winchester.

Tears were in Jeremiah's eyes; the creature had fallen, but it was too late. Sasha was laying out on the ground, a gaping wound stretched from her right shoulder, across her neck, and up to her left ear. Her eyes were wide; he never studied her eyes until now; they were the color of leaves that fell in the fall. He slowly saw a slight glaze spreading over them. She looked so calm and collected, almost as if nothing were wrong.

Jeremiah ran over, kneeling down; applying pressure to her jugular as Marie began to cry out in horror and distress. Everything went blurry, he could feel the blood pulsing through his fingers. He cried with anger, upset; trying to save the life of someone he hardly knew. He had broken his promise; she wasn't getting home safe.

She looked up at Jeremiah, a half smile came through the blood, but her eyes told the smile was meant to be full. She lifted up a hand as Marie rushed over. Marie grasped her hand tightly, crying, her face contorted in the deepest emotional pain. Sasha looked over at her sister, giving her the same smile she gave Jeremiah.

"N-now… Marie…" she attempted to speak through the blood. "T-t-tell mom I, I'm-m s-sorry. B-b-b-but make s-sure you tell her." She looked over at Jeremiah, harsh pain flickered in her eyes. She took her free hand and began to meekly play with the opal necklace. "M-my m-mother gave this-this to me. You should t-take it to h-her. P-please, keep Marie s-s-safe."

"I will." He replied, yet the words were almost non-existent through tears. He looked into her eyes once more, watching the life flash quickly out of them. Her hand holding her sisters began to slip and fall to the earth, but Marie refused to let it go; she grasped with both of her hands, pressing her forehead against the lifeless fingertips.

Jeremiah scooted around Sasha to hold Marie by the shoulders. He tried to pull her away, but she fought him; scrambling back to her sister, crying out her name. Jeremiah pulled her in close, attempting to calm her, "There's nothin we can do."

"No! Why wasn't I given with the power to heal? To bring life back into a body? I can't leave her out here, not here, not here… You said you'd help us! We were supposed to get home safe, together. Why did this happen? Why...? We can't leave her here!"

"We won't, we'll bury her." Marie continued to sob and fight Jeremiah, trying to get back to the side of her sister. He felt a lump in his throat, swelling larger and larger with each breath he took. He couldn't swallow, it was as if he were drowning in his tears.

CHAPTER 7

There was a new mark in the map; a simple cross drawn with *Sasha* written above it. The new mark on the map was perfectly set in between the Church they had slept in and a small *h* that Jeremiah assumed was the girls home. Jeremiah played with the opal necklace inside his pocket, maybe for comfort as the prayer he had said over that poor girl's lonely grave echoed in his head over and over again:

Lord, take this child's soul into your paradise. Find her peace, allow her to rest with her father among the angels. Although her life was taken too soon, we understand that you have a plan. In the name of the father, the son the holy spirit. Amen.

Each step he took seemed heavier than the last; he had failed one of them while attempting to protect them both. Marie's head was hanging low as she tried to keep up with his heavy strides. He could feel the pain that seemed to radiate from her small body. He felt destroyed, yet not defeated.

The fog never let up, they sky seemed to darken more so with every hundred or so steps Jeremiah took. He stopped at one point to make sure Marie was alright; or as alright as one could be. He lit a cigarette. The tobacco soothed him just enough to where he could think straight for the first time since Sasha had fallen. As he inhaled its precious toxin he came to the realization that there was no more time to stop, no more time to eat or sleep; he had to get Marie home and the opal necklace to her mother. He walked over to the sled and grabbed the last bit of water from it. He took a short sip and put it in his satchel. He grabbed the rope and again began his heavy footsteps; smoke trailing behind them from his lit cigarette.

Marie began to trail behind at some point, Jeremiah tried to slow to a pace where she could keep up, but she kept slowing. He looked at her, seeing her eyelids had begun a decent to sleep. He stopped and picked her up, putting her on his back with her arms over his shoulders, her legs under his hands; she fell asleep almost instantly. He continued to pull the sled behind them as he tried to walk as smoothly as possible so as to not wake Marie. He knew she could have laid down on the sled, but he felt that he would rather be able to see her; just in case something happened.

The walk was long, and although he vowed to not stop until Marie was safe in her mother's arms, there were a few times they had to stop for various reasons. Sometimes he heard rustling nearby, sometimes Marie would wake up and decide to walk for a bit. Just as he had begun to feel sleep reach its long fingers into his mind, the sky seemed to begin to light up; visibility increased through the mist with every step. Then, off in the distance, he could see the outline of a small settlement. Lights of candles and fires shone through mismatched windows above a small fence. It was still darker than the bridge he had stayed on, but lighter than when he encountered Whisper.

He tapped Marie on the shoulder; she had been looking down at her feet the entire time she walked. She looked up and Jeremiah could see her eyes light up with hope and anticipation. She ran out ahead; calling out "Mommy! Mommy! I'm home!"

Jeremiah chased after her, almost losing his step as he pulled the sled behind him. Marie kept calling out, the closer she got the louder she would yell. There was some commotion coming from the houses, and then Jeremiah heard a woman's voice from a crowd scream with excitement, "Marie!"

Jeremiah felt relief and excitement in his heart, he slowed to watch Marie embrace her mother. Even in the dim light, he could see tears of joy fall from her mother's eyes.

"Oh, Marie!" The woman said brushing her auburn hair out of her face, "I was so worried, you were supposed to be home days ago!" She kept a tight grip on her daughter, sobbing slightly, "Where is your sister? Where's daddy?"

Jeremiah's blood ran cold as arctic waters, and he froze in his tracks; he had known he would have to encounter a mother and have to deliver destroying news. He contemplated how to go about it, trying to figure out the best way to approach her. Before he could take another step forward Marie relieved him of that burden.

"Mom... Daddy couldn't find someone to take us back home..."

"What about the couriers we hired?" Her mother looked at her child, watching her shake her head *no*, "So they took you, and then just dumped you there? Did the surgery go well at least?"

Marie pulled down the collar of her shirt slightly, revealing a scar just below her collarbone to her mother; Jeremiah was unable to see the scar from his vantage point, but could read the small amount of relief on her mother's face. Then, through tears, Marie continued, "Daddy tried to find a safe way home, he really tried, but no one would help. So, he made a sled, and we started walking. We walked so far mom..."

49

"You *walked*?"

"Yes… and some men came out of nowhere… they… they…" Marie buried her face into her mother's chest, telling her mother what happened to their father. Although her voice was muffled, Jeremiah could hear some of the words; "Grabbed daddy… pushed… took the sled… shot… We were alone, mommy…" Then Marie looked up and pointed at Jeremiah, "Then he came over, we were scared. He went after the men and brought the sled back. He lives in a pickup truck. He told us he'd get us home, and he got me home…" Marie stopped talking, looking up at her mother, and then to Jeremiah.

Jeremiah stepped forward, producing the small opal necklace from his duster pocket. He held it out for the mother to take, but she was frozen with pain piercing her eyes. "I'm sorry," Jeremiah said softly, "I told 'em I'd protect 'em, and I did all I could, I promise yo-"

"Where is my daughter?" She hollered, "What happened to her? Where is she? Where *is* she?" She stepped toward Jeremiah, close enough to snatch the necklace that hung from his outstretched hand. She fell over, face contoured in pain, releasing silent cries. Her chest heaved, shoulders shuttering up and then down. Jeremiah went to comfort the mother, but she lurched up and swung feebly at his side. It made contact with just enough force to make Jeremiah back away as she continued to swing.

"Where is my daughter? Where is she?"

A man who was watching the reunion from the front of a makeshift home had rushed over to restrain the grieving woman. "Go away!" She cried out to Jeremiah as the man held her. The commotion had drawn the other residents of the small settlement to help.

Another man took Jeremiah by the shoulder and led him away from the mother and Marie. Jeremiah looked back, catching Marie's sorrowful gaze as if to apologize to him; it trapped a fresh stone in his throat. The man led Jeremiah into a small building, closing the door behind them. Even through the closed door, he could hear the mother crying out; her pain penetrated him as he found the closest chair.

Jeremiah sat, hunched in the chair; hand on his brow while his elbow rested on a distressed wood table. He was staring directly at the table, but his mind was somewhere else. He was not thinking about the countless water rings left by long empty glasses, not paying attention to the scratches and scrapes that had taken away the sheen the old table clearly once had. No, his mind was nowhere near that table, it was focused on the poor woman grieving out in the streets with her daughter. Those tears she shed softly patted against the dusty ground, each one landed to fling a few molecules of dirt up into the stale air. It killed Jeremiah.

A small glass of whiskey was placed down next to his elbow. If it weren't for the fact that he knew he needed a drink he wouldn't have even noticed its presence.

"House brew, apparently." A man's voice said, "They say they make it here when they have the stuff to make it. This one is on me."

"Wastin' your cut, eh Gunny?" A woman's voice called out before Jeremiah even looked up.

"Piss off!" The man's voice called out, "Looks like this guy's had a rougher day than us."

He heard the woman laugh, "Yea! Well, I don't see him with scars on him from those damn Count-Hounds…"

"*Cont*-Hounds, moron, just stick to navigating and shut the hell up!" The man sat down next to Jeremiah, putting a hand on his shoulder to comfort him. Jeremiah looked up to see a young man, maybe in his early twenties. He had thick black hair combed back by sweat and grime, his stubble had small particles of dirt caught within the barely growing beard. His eyes seemed kind, yet battle-hardened the way he had seen in the eyes of young men who came home when the war had come to a close. The man extended his free hand to Jeremiah, "Names Tom," he began, "I'm the gunner of the crew, so they just been calling me *Gunny* for the longest time."

For a moment, Jeremiah wanted to give a false name but was unable to produce a reasonable replacement for his own. "Jeremiah." He said, taking Toms hand and giving him the firmest handshake he could with what little energy he had left. He looked down at the glass, then back at Tom. "Gunner? Crew?" he asked wearily, using almost all the strength he could muster just to find his voice.

"Well, damn; I figured you'd been in this shit for a while. Sorry." Tom gestured at Jeremiah's glass, beckoning him to take at least one sip.

Jeremiah did, savoring the amber liquid as it burned down into his empty stomach. He coughed a little, but not enough to make him not want more.

"So, you haven't encountered any Couriers before?" Tom asked once Jeremiahs glass had once more reached the table.

"Can't say I have, then again I haven't been here that long."

Jeremiah grunted, "Heard Ma-" He stopped himself, he didn't know this man and had no intention of giving him Marie's name. "Heard that lil' girl and her mom sayin' somethin' 'bout Couriers."

"Yea, well, to make it short; it's a group of people who travel from place to place bringing supplies and doing jobs as they're needed. Sometimes it's dangerous, sometimes it's easy; mostly dangerous. Hell, some towns have their own designated couriers because they aren't on any route. Those guys are the lucky ones."

"Huh," Jeremiah didn't really know what to make of what Tom was saying, and he honestly didn't care much. His whiskey still sat in front of him, unfinished; his right index figure played with the rim of the glass while he contemplated his next gulp.

"Anyway, you said you survived out there; hell, you walked Gods know how long. What I'm trying to say is: maybe we could use another lookout or gunner." He turned to face the woman he had been yelling at earlier, "Isn't that right, Carol?"

"The hell are you rambling about over there, Gunny?" She called back, obviously not hearing the conversation Jeremiah and Tom had just had. She seemed to be a little bit too preoccupied attempting to get the two men who sat at the table behind her to buy her a few drinks; maybe even a nice bed to have some quality time. She waved off Tom's response before he even had the chance to open his mouth, "Whatever. Why don't you go talk to the Driver or something; I'm just a bit busy." She turned back to the two men behind her.

Tom turned back to Jeremiah, gesturing at his glass once more, "Well, finish up your drink and we can go talk to Driver if you want. Least we can do is maybe drop you off at the next settlement or something."

Jeremiah thought about Tom's proposal as he stared at the glass of whiskey. He gripped it slightly, and in one single motion, shot it down. "Well," he said after letting out a short sigh, "I suppose it wouldn't be a bad idea to get somewhere; anywhere. I just d-"

"Alright!" Tom clapped Jeremiah on the back, "Well, we should head over to the store where Driver is, and then we can get you onboard." He stood up, Jeremiah followed, "Oh, and by the way, some places will accept just about any currency you got; but chances are you gotta barter. Figured you'd like to know, just in case." Tom left a small folded up bill as well as two bullets on the table before leading Jeremiah out the old wooden door.

Jeremiah found himself staring at a large vehicle; it had four lights on the front with an old and rusted silver grate. The back was large, but it was cramped due to all the supplies that it had. There was a makeshift ladder on the right corner inside of the large back; it led up to a small hole just large enough for a man to fit through. On the top was a large weapon attached to a pivoting and rotating stand.

Tom talked about the vehicle, that he called a *Rig* for a moment, but Jeremiah could barely understand a word of it. "You see, it's some old moving van we found. Needed a bit of cleaning, but it wasn't hard to get it to run again. The cab connects to the back through a large metal pipe we found, and I tell you it was an absolute bitch to install without a welder, but it's solid. If you can shoot a fifty-cal, it's up top; just make sure you save the bullets, they are hard to come by. Don't worry, though, usually, I'm the one up top." Tom pointed to a corner where four bunks were attached to the side, "You can lay your stuff on the top bunk."

Jeremiah looked at him, a thousand questions running through his head but he was too tired to figure out what to ask first. He simply nodded and placed his satchel on the top bunk. He held his pistol in one hand, juggling with the idea of placing it there or keeping it on him. He decided just until he could get comfortable with the crew it would be a good idea to not let any of his weapons leave his side.

"So, the Cowboy from the bar is hitching a ride?" A familiar female voice said from behind them. Jeremiah turned to see the Carol – who Tom had explained was the navigator – climbing into the back of the rig. She threw her effects on the bunk just below Jeremiah's, then she extended a hand out to him, "Names Carol."

"Jeremiah." He said, taking her hand in a meek handshake.

Carol laughed "Well, I hope that handshake isn't a sign of your character, or I'd say we dump you right now." She began to walk away, but not before giving him a quick slap on the left buttock.

Jeremiah didn't know how to react; he just turned at watched her start to climb through the tube that connected the cab to the back. As soon as she was out of sight, her head re-emerged from the small hole, blowing a kiss and winking at Jeremiah before disappearing once more. Before he could say anything to Tom, he heard an unfamiliar voice from behind him.

"Eh," The voice began, thick in an accent Jeremiah could again not place, "Someone, eh, new? Yes?" Jeremiah turned to see not a human, but a very tall creature. He had a face similar to a human, except the proportions were all off; small slit for a mouth, a single nostril with no nose, and two large hexagonal eyes that reflected almost everything in the field of view. It wore no clothing, and its skin was scaly with an orange-brown hue.

Jeremiah quickly recoiled, his back against the bunks and his hand on the pistol at his hip; his eyes were wide with fear.

"Woah!" Tom called out, putting himself between Jeremiah and the creature, "Now, this is just our lookout. We call him Zed." Tom leaned in and whispered to Jeremiah, "Don't ask him his actual name; you won't understand anything he says, trust me."

Zed blinked, only a single eyelid on each eye jetted upwards from the bottom for a split second before returning. He extended a hand that seemed to have no fingers, only claws before recoiling it back to his side. "I'm, eh, soy-ee. I fogot that, eh…" He trailed off, mumbling in some screeching language, "But, yes, I Zed. Nice to, eh, meet you!" A smile, or what looked like a smile, appeared on Zed's lips before he hopped effortlessly into the confined space.

Jeremiah looked at Tom who gave him a comforting smile. "Don't worry, Zed is completely harmless. Well, mostly harmless."

"Yes, eh… Don think I mean…" Zed trailed off again, trying to remember the English words he needed, "You am good, I no hut you."

"Sorry," Tom said, "He can't pronounce an *r* for some reason, though he'll learn; right, Zed?"

Jeremiah tipped his hat slightly, mouth still agape in inappreciable fear, "Nice to meet you, uhh, Zed."

Zed's smile came back, just before he disappeared up the makeshift ladder and onto the roof. Jeremiah felt exhausted, more so than he did before; it was a lot to take in on such little sleep. He hoped that Driver would arrive soon, so they could get on their way out of this small town and away from his failure. He pictured the large, mostly out of shape man that the crew simply referred to as Driver. They had a brief meeting in a store, but Driver paid no attention to Jeremiah as he was trying to make a deal with the short woman behind the counter. He remembered Tom talking to the man for a short time before ushering Jeremiah over to this so-called rig.

Tom could see Jeremiah getting more and more tired, and gave him a quick pat on the back. "Get some rest, we'll be heading out soon; just sleep now." Tom gave Jeremiah a half smile before leaving him alone in the back of the rig.

Jeremiah tried to contemplate how he ended up in the back of this rig as he climbed his way onto the top bunk. He lay there for a moment, staring off at the half rusted steel that was inches away from his face. Something about the rig reminded him so much of sleeping in the pickup truck on that bridge, and then he remembered Sasha's face and voice.

Something inside of him gripped at his heart and lungs, making it hard to breathe; a lump once again formed in his throat and Jeremiah knew that only a large amount of whiskey would help it go away. Instead, he surrendered himself to the sweetness of sleep.

Everything was white; no sound or landscape, just white. Jeremiah remembered something similar to this but was still too tired to remember anything at all. He turned, observing all around him; nothing. Then, suddenly, felt a sudden burst of air.

Instead of the white nothingness, he was standing in a cabin, made from salvaged supplies and materials. There was a single table in the middle of the room, one chair, and nothing more. The scene outside the window looked oddly familiar, and then he realized where he was; back in the town he had recently left.

"Hello Jeremiah," A small and familiar voice said from behind him. He turned around to see Marie sitting in the chair. "I'm sorry about everything."

"Nothing was your fault, it was mine." He responded, choking on his words.

"No, it wasn't. You did everything you could. You are such a good man. I'm sorry about my Mom, she was just upset. I know she thanks you for being able to get me home, I saw it in her mind, I know it.."

"But I promised to get ya' both home, and I didn't." Jeremiah could feel that lump in his throat once more, heavier and much coarser than he had remembered from when he was awake. Tears came like a flood, drawing the life out of him.

Marie walked over and hugged him, soaking his tears in her hair and blouse. She hushed him as he put his arms around her and squeezed her. "You did great. You saved me, you did all you could to save her, you are such a good man. I want to thank you, I wish I could give you any gift you want, but I can't."

Jeremiah looked up into her deep eyes, though everything in his field of vision was a blur. He stroked her hair and forced a smile. "No, no, you don't owe me a thing; just live on and take care of your mom. Grow up, do some good. You're a smart kid, a good kid; use it."

"I am using it, using it to tell you; thank you. I'm using it to tell you that my mother thanks you. I'm using it to make sure you understand what you did for me." She sighed, her head began to hang low, "I'm using it... using it to make sure you understand that it isn't all your fault."

Jeremiah closed his eyes, picturing Sasha before she fell; she is playing with her necklace, walking next to him. He could see her black hair bobbing up and down as she stepped forward with him. She looked up and her eyes seemed to pop out against the gray dullness around her. Those eyes were so young, full of life; she looked happy as she walked with him. She smiled, then looked back ahead. Jeremiah turned to see what she was seeing; nothing. Ahead was just the mist as it once was. His eyes opened.

"Sasha," he began, "She didn't even get a chance. I could've saved her; I know I could've. I should have done so much more for you two; the hell type of man am I? I can't save a soul."

Marie looked at him, half perplexed, half concerned. "No, you did all you could. I know about Whisper."

Jeremiah's eyes grew wide, terrified of the repercussions of even talking to a so-called God. He pictured finding a way to shoot that woman down, then forcing her to bring Sasha back to the world.

"Stop thinking that," Marie said, "You did everything to protect us; I mean it. She would understand, she would thank you for not giving me up to Whisper. Daddy said that someone may want me one day, and if so I should never go. You did exactly what you should have done." She wrapped her arms around him once more, squeezing tighter than a 5-year-old should be able to. He closed his eyes, listening to her voice, "And I'm glad you didn't go. Sasha would thank you; and I'm sure she does thank you; Just like I thank you, and Mommy thanks you... Thank you, Jeremiah, thank you."

Jeremiah felt her grip loosen until he couldn't feel her arms around him any longer. He opened his eyes to see the pure nothingness the dream had begun with. He wondered for a while, contemplating nothing; only relaxing in the knowledge he had helped someone. For the first time since Sasha had died, he felt like he had done the right thing.

CHAPTER 8

Jeremiah was jostled awake by the jerking and bumping of the rig; he could hear the great roar of it as they sped forward and off into the Grey. Jeremiah wondered how long they'd been traveling, he still felt slightly drowsy and wondered if he needed more rest. His head slowly swayed side to side as he stared up at the never changing rusted steel above his head, making out shapes and images where the paint had peeled. He wondered if the structure was sound with the amount of rust in his view, but shook the thought off; if this structure wasn't sound, then how would it be able to move at what felt like such a high speed?

Jeremiah forced himself out of his bunk, crashing his feet against the steel floor with a thud. His head felt lighter than air, his stomach empty, he struggled to maintain footing inside of the moving vehicle. He studied the inside of the vehicle; it was roughly seven or so feet tall, seven feet wide, and maybe about thirteen or so feet in length. There was a small crawls space at the end where Driver and Carol must be. Almost every inch of space was filled with boxes and other loose items. There was plenty of rust around and he could tell that someone had attempted to fix some of it, but probably gave up or ran out of supplies.

Some random objects were strewn about; empty water containers, a few large crates that read *Food Stuffs* or *Medical*, some random ammunition, and some personal effects.

There were so many unmarked crates that Jeremiah didn't know exactly why it was all needed.

The rig hit a large bump, making Jeremiah stumble and fall to his knees. The cold of the steel penetrated through his pants, his knees sending the chill through the rest of his body.

He regained his composure, and stood back up; he heard voices over the wind noise from above him. He made his way over to the ladder and climbed it, having to push open a heavy hatch at the top. There he found Zed and Tom sitting on top of the rig talking to each other. There was railing along the sides to make sure they didn't fall off from the speed.

Jeremiah looked over to Tom, who still had not noticed his presence as he was trying to explain to Zed the sound of an *R*. He could see Zed doing his best, but the only sounds that came out were not of this world. Jeremiah attempted to light a cigarette, but to no avail. The sounds of a match striking against paper made Zed come aware of

Jeremiah's presence. He glanced over to shoot Jeremiah a small smile before returning to his lesson.

Jeremiah did his best to not interrupt, but his stomach was empty, and he needed something to settle it. He reached over and tapped Tom on the shoulder. Tom looked over to Jeremiah and smiled, "Well, you're up after a good few hours. You missed all the fun!"

Jeremiah didn't know what he meant by that, nor did he want to know what had happened while he was asleep, all he wanted was something to settle his stomach. "Got somethin' to eat? I'm starvin'."

Tom reached into his pocket and pulled out a small bar wrapped in silver paper and handed it to Jeremiah. On the paper, it simply was labeled *Energy PluS+*, followed by several numbers and percent signs. "Here, energy bar. This is from way after your time. Essentially it is in case of emergency, like you're stranded and don't have anything substantial to eat. One bar is supposed to be a full meal of energy and what-have-you. I recommend eating half of it; it tastes like crap. You should probably stay up here and keep watch, though, wouldn't be a bad idea to earn your keep." Tom turned and went back to his conversation with Zed.

Jeremiah opened the small bar of food; it couldn't be more than three or four bites for him to finish it off, but he decided to listen to Tom and only eat half. He tore off a section of the bar and then re-wrapped the other part and put it in his satchel. He took a bite; Tom was right, it tasted and *felt* like eating dust. Jeremiah almost coughed at the feeling of his mouth drying out from what should be a survival item, and he felt his need for water would outweigh anything that the rig had. Fortunately, the thirst quickly subsided and Jeremiah's stomach began to feel full. Something about the bar just felt chemical to him, but it did the job it was supposed to do. When he finished he found himself an area to sit and began to look out onto the road.

To him, everything seemed to be the same; white-grey mist swirling about, obstructing any possible line of sight to any destination. Not even hills nor trees could be seen in the distance through the thickness, and it made Jeremiah long for those Texas skies he had grown to love.

Maybe these were the Texas skies, hidden by the soup that encased the world. He lit a cigarette, cautiously in the wind, as if it were the days long past on his porch.

The rig jolted before slowing down to a complete stop. Metal on metal could be heard as it decelerated at a small building that stood in complete disrepair. Strips of green and white paint were peeling from the exterior as bark from a maple tree. Broken windows reflected the light from the rig. Atop the structure was a sign that couldn't be read thanks to the bullet holes and scrapes across its face. Four small structures stood in front of the main buildings broken windows, fully erect, faded to white. Jeremiah scanned the structure for any signs of life or importance; nothing.

"Gunny!" Drivers voice called up from his seat in the rig, "Do you see anything from up there?"

"Not a thing; all clear."

"You and that damn cowboy keep on watch. I need Zed to try to get some of this damn gasoline out of these pumps. See anything, yell out, and we'll get the hell out of here." The rig jolted back to life, pulled up to one of the small structures in front of the main building.

Jeremiah heard some shuffling from inside the rig, then the massive door opened at the rear. Zed stood up to his full six-and-a-half-foot height, allowing a single stride to bring him over the railing, and then he vanished off the side of the rig.

Tom reached an arm across Jeremiah's face, pointing off into the distance, "You keep a lookout over there," he then pointed in the opposite direction, "I'll watch that way. You see anything, let me know." Tom made his way to the rear of the rig and scanned the thick air, intense eyes looking out for anything that may approach.

From all that Jeremiah could see, the ground looked as if it were battle scarred; small craters randomly scattered throughout the terrain with debris speckling other points.

Something just didn't sit right with him about this area, the air gave a faint smell of death; or maybe it was just the air that was dead. The only sound that he heard was the mechanical tinkering by Zed and the occasional groan or grunt by Driver. He did his best to ignore it and try to focus on the task of making sure nothing was approaching.

It caught Jeremiah's eye, off in the distance, as if a shadow had simply moved on its own accord. He darted his eyes in the direction of the movement; nothing. He whistled, trying to get Tom's attention. Tom walked over to him in a crouch, as if trying to hide from an unseen enemy on the field. "Over there, saw something move," Jeremiah pointed out in the direction he was looking, "But nothin's there."

"You sure?"

"Unless you see somethin', cause all it looked like was a shadow wi-"

Tom called down to the team on the ground; "Got shadows moving! Might want to hurry the hell up before they decide to move some more!" He turned to Jeremiah, "Good job; if you see any more movement you tell them, and we'll get going." Tom made his way in the same crouch back to the other side of the rig, his eyes sweeping back and forth.

Jeremiah continued to look out, his heart pounding in his ears, not allowing him to hear the sheer silence of his surroundings. He tried to focus on any area where there may be a creature or person hiding, any area where light could be casting a shadow. He kept feeling like something would soon move out of the corner of his eye, but for several minutes it was as still as the dead. His eyes began to dry from forcing his eyes to stay open.

"Got shadows moving!" Tom cried out to the team on the ground, "Let's get going, now!"

Jeremiah heard a click followed by a loud, concussing blast. His ears started ringing, Jeremiah pressed his palms against the side of his head. He looked up to see Zed climbing over the side of the rig, pulling a small canister from a belt. He used a massive claw to pull a small key from the side, and then threw the canister over Jeremiah's head. There was another loud sound of thunder, as he saw Zed light up from what he could only assume was lightning. He felt the rig rumble, and then he began to lose his footing as it began to lurch forward away from the lonely building.

Tom grabbed Jeremiah by the shoulder, pulling him to his feet while simultaneously pressing a cylinder into his hands. He leaned in, "You see any shadows in the next ten minutes, you pull that damn pin and throw it at them!" Tom pointed to a small loop towards the top of the cylinder and then returned to his place on top of the rig.

The rig jolted and jumped, groaning under the speed it was fleeing at. Jeremiah had to sometimes shield his eyes from the wind as it whipped against his face. It was hard for him to tell if anything was moving as he couldn't figure if it was just the jostling from the speeding rig. He tried to concentrate on anything, everything, but it all sped by too quickly for him to understand. Something came over him, a feeling of helplessness; loss. Jeremiah closed his eyes to bring himself back to reality; he breathed deeply, focusing on whatever was rambling around in his mind. Just then, the air rushed out of his lungs as he felt a sharp pain pierce his chest.

He looked down to see a dark, transparent hand reaching into his chest. He could feel it grip at his heart, squeezing tight, forcing the blood to no longer flow. Jeremiah was immobilized with fear as he saw nothing but a shadow before him; his own shadow.

His vision began to blur, his line of sight began to tunnel, he knew this was the end. Without warning, he heard a loud crash accompanied by a bright flash. Jeremiah couldn't see, and the only sound he could make out was a ringing in his ear, but at least his heart had been released. He began to pat at his chest, unable to see his hands as he did, noting protruded out; no signs of injury.

He felt a hand on his shoulder and immediately went to swing in the direction he had believed it came from. Whatever he swung at was nowhere near his fist as all it connected with was the thick air. He went to swing again but stopped as his sight began to come back. Though the figure was still blurry, he knew it was Tom who had gone to his side. Lips were moving in what Jeremiah could only conceive was a coherent sentence, but all he could hear was the metallic whistle that bounced through his ears.

Jeremiah was still shaken from the encounter with shadows only a few hours before, he had rummaged through his belongings to scrounge out a pack of *Camel* cigarettes. Though he didn't prefer them, he knew it would be easier than rolling his own cigarette in the moving rig. He didn't have the nerve to poke his head back to the top, he preferred the safety of the four rusting steel walls around him; at least for the moment.

Jeremiah was no coward, but he couldn't shake the fact that his own shadow was a demon waiting to attack.

Well, at least that is the way Tom made it out to be.

According to Tom, those creatures were once the children of a new God. He said that the God went mad over the never ending twilight he was forced to live in, and thrust his children onto mankind in order to collect their souls. Souls, at least to this god, were light.

The tobacco was a savior, once again; he watched the smoke drift up to the ceiling and out the open hatch.

Although he had rested for more hours than he actually knew the night before, the encounter not only left him shaken but exhausted beyond comprehension. He knew this was no time for sleep now; Tom told him to take a twenty-minute break before he wanted him back for watch, this was mostly due to Jeremiah's jittering nerves causing his rifle to shake with every shadow he saw. Jeremiah considered the idea of taking a short nap, but no matter how exhausted he may have felt; his mind was buzzing with ways to comprehend what had happened. Again, he inhaled his sweet poison; holding it for a moment in his lungs before releasing a small cloud off into the back of the rig.

He sat on one of the crates and just tried to think about something good, something familiar. But, alas, nothing good nor familiar could come to his distraught mind.

He could overhear Driver and Carol discussing fuel and the next stop they had to make. Driver seemed convinced they had enough fuel to make it; although just barely. Carol seemed to think they would be stranded in the middle of nowhere. She raised her voice, cursing, and complaining, and then he couldn't hear her anymore. Shortly after their argument had ended, he heard some shuffling before Carol came out of the opening connecting the front of the rig to the back.

"Jeff is just such a git!" she proclaimed as soon as she noticed Jeremiah sitting in the back, "Damn fool thinks there's enough gasoline to make it out to Galveston settlement; damn clot!" She made her way over to Jeremiah, sitting down on a crate to face him. She eyed his cigarette and took a deep breath of the smoke swirling out of the rig, "Got an extra one of those?"

Jeremiah walked over to his bunk and grabbed the pack of *Camel* cigarettes out of his satchel. He fumbled them around as the rig hit a large bump, but was able to keep hold with his callus fingers. He made his way carefully over to Carol, holding the pack of cigarettes in an outstretched hand. She took the pack and pulled one out slowly before tossing the pack back to Jeremiah. As he put the pack in his front pocket, he noticed Carol taking a long whiff of the unlit cigarette.

Eventually she placed it in her lips, lit it, and reclined against the wall. Through a thick billow, she sighed, "Wish this wasn't how it was."

Jeremiah looked at her, puzzled as if to ask what she meant. He realized there was no way she could see anything through the swirls of sweet burning tobacco smoke around her, "What ya' mean by that?"

"Get picked up cause somehow you know your way around this damn-" she made a swirling gesture with one hand while the other brought the cigarette to her lips for another taste of its calming toxins, "whatever the hell you want to call it. Just never thought this is what life had in store for me, that's all." She looked down at her feet for a moment, as of waiting for a thoughtful response to her concerns.

"I don't think anyone saw this shit-storm comin', not even close," Jeremiah wanted to offer a hand on her shoulder but stopped himself short. He didn't want to make her think everything was going to be alright; he didn't want to give some false hope that a simple kind gesture could conjure inside of someone, "But, *He* has a plan for all of us."

She looked up at him, almost angry as she sat straight and pointed the hot ember as an extension of her own hand in his direction. "You think *He* gives two shits and a fuck about us? And exactly what *He* are you referring to. Don't know if anyone told you this, cowboy, but there's a shit load of God's out there all trying to keep their share of humanity. Fuck, what do you think attacked us at that gas station?"

She jolted up, coming nose to nose with Jeremiah.

"I didn't mean nothin by it, just-"

"No, you don't get it!" Her voice was raising over the constant hum in the rig, he could smell the cigarette fresh on her breath. "We've all been praying, every last one of us, to whatever God or Goddess we know. They don't give a shit! Hell, you can walk with them now, you can *kill* them now, so what makes you think *He* has some great plan for us *now*?"

Jeremiah tried to find the words to calm Carol down, but couldn't; he could only focus on the fact that the mere mention of *any* God made her explode in a rage. He could see small beads of sweat beginning to roll down her brow and to her nose. He didn't know whether to be frightened or infuriated by her outburst but decided he should just back down before they threw him out the door and leave him in the middle of nowhere.

"Carol, get back to the front!" Tom was coming down from the top of the rig, eyes fixed on the outraged woman, "Leave him alone; whatever he did to piss you off, he didn't mean it!"

Carol never broke eye contact with Jeremiah. She took a drag off her cigarette before blowing it into Jeremiah's face and leaving through the opening at the front of the rig. He stood there, confused and bothered by the entire encounter. He fell backward to sit on the crate he had originally claimed and took his final inhale of tobacco.

Tom came over, slapped Jeremiah on the shoulder as he sat next to him. "Sorry about her… but what did she get so upset about?"

"God," Jeremiah replied in a short exhale of smoke.

"Ah, yeah, that will definitely do it." Tom leaned back against the wall, "Yea, she had some problems with her deity a while back. Don't worry too much about it, just don't do it again."

"Alright, I'll do my damn best not to."

"Well, how about you get back up there so I can take a bit of a rest." He got up and started to walk to his bunk, "Grab me in maybe thirty minutes or so."

The rig came to a complete stop just outside the Galveston settlement. Another small building was next to them with 4 stalls, faded and in disarray, but this one was lit by what appeared to be small candles in the windows. Jeremiah watched as Jeff (Driver) got out of the vehicle followed by Carol. He looked triumphant, almost cocky as he talked to Carol about the fuel.

The settlement was still about 100 yards away, but the fog was not as thick as it usually was so he could see faint figures moving around the streets with candles and lanterns. Some of the people appeared to be watching the rig while others just looked to be going about their daily lives.

"Alright!" Jeff called up to Jeremiah, Tom, and Zed. His voice was rough, not exactly battle hardened; rather rough much the way a sailor sounds after navigating stormy waters. "They'll be fillin' 'er up. We got some crates needing to go to the general store, and someone else is apparently lookin' for a group to do a job. I'll meet with them after we get paid for this one, so let's move."

Jeremiah and Tom climbed one by one down the small ladder into the rig, Zed just bounded over the edge and entered through the back. When Jeremiah's feet touched the steel floor Zed had already slung one crate over his shoulder and was pulling the other behind him out of the rig. Jeremiah located the last crate and went to lift it.

It was much heavier than expected, and Jeremiah could only let out a grunt before huffing in defeat.

"Woah!" Tom said grabbing one of the handles, "This thing is at least 200 kilos, possibly a bit more." He nodded in the direction of the other handle and waited for Jeremiah to take hold of it, "Alright; one, two, three!"

The two men grunted in unison as they lifted the crate. It was still heavy with the weight split between the two of them, and Jeremiah could see Tom was having as much trouble as he was. They waddled over to the edge of the rig and set it down. Tom went over to the side of the rig, waving for Jeremiah to follow him. On the right side of the rig was a small latch with a *U*-shaped ring holding it in place. It connected to a piece of metal that went under the rig itself, holding something in place.

"So," Tom began, "I'm going to crawl under there and undo the first latch. When I say, then you undo this latch." Tom crawled under the rig, grunting as his back scooted along the ground. After a brief moment of metallic bangs and clanks, he called out to Jeremiah. "Undo the latch!"

Jeremiah undid the latch, and a small cart dropped down from the underside of the rig. It was made of tubular steel and had thick black wheels. Tom crawled out from under the rig and pulled the cart out with him. He pulled up a handle that was lying flat on the top of the cart until he heard a loud *click*. "This will make it much easier than carrying." He said with a half-smile, "Let's just get it to it's new owner, then we can grab ourselves a drink."

Jeremiah smiled back at Tom, *good,* he thought to himself, *I already finished off the last of my whiskey.*

CHAPTER 9

Jeremiah's satchel was heavier as they were leaving the Galveston settlement than when they had first arrived. He had obtained some more *Camel* cigarettes, except this time they were in a green box instead of a blue and white one, a small bottle of whiskey, a small bottle of local alcohol made from fermented grapefruit, and an extra canteen with water. He also had the jingle of twelve gold pieces and some small silver coins; it had originally just been sixteen gold pieces, but he needed his own supplies.

Galveston smelled of a rotting ocean mixed with burning coal. Yet, to him, it seemed like something completely different; none of the buildings were in total disarray, though some did show wear from the ocean winds. He tried to figure when they were actually built but gave up after some time of finding random switches and holes in the walls. The windows would stay open without having to be propped, and the streets were like the lonesome bridge he stayed on. It felt strange to him, and it was still Texas.

But, now he was away from that; back on the rig sitting on the floor where a supply crate used to be. A fresh hand-rolled cigarette was lit in one hand, and a half-empty flask weighed in the other.

He contemplated everything that had happened in the few days he had spent in the Grey; pondering the meaning of it all. *Was this Hell? Was this purgatory? Was this all for some unseen sin? A dream with no ending?* These thoughts along with many more danced around his head in a chaotic tango of sorrow. Something didn't settle right in his stomach – and it wasn't the whiskey – making him feel somewhat sick and groggy, though he couldn't exactly figure just what it was.

The rig came to a sudden stop, jerking him forward; almost causing him to spill the open flask. As soon as he regained balance he heard Jeff yelling at Carol; "What do you mean *he* hired us on this job? You know Tlaloc still hasn't paid us for the last job we ran for him? Are you mental?"

"Well, this one seems easy," Carol replied, "We have the intel, he just needs to meet us in person for it. We wait until he pays us for *both* jobs, and only *then* does he get the information."

"But we have another damn job! We have to run over to Athens and get water to run to Dallas! When, exactly, do you expect us to make it all the way out there in order to meet with that damn freeloader?"

Dallas; now Jeremiah knew that name, but unfortunately, could not figure out the way without the help of the couriers.

The rig began to move again, drowning out any further debate that Jeff and Carol may have been having. He decided to climb up to the top to join Zed and Tom; make sure that he earned his pay for whatever job they had coming.

Tom and Zed seemed completely focused on the nothing that surrounded them, not turning to acknowledge Jeremiah even with the loud thud from the closing hatch. He decided not to even attempt to make conversation; he felt he had nothing to really discuss with the two of them that they didn't already know. As he took his position facing forward, everything froze around him. He instinctually put a hand on his sidearm; he knew who was coming.

"Hello, Jeremiah." A familiar voice said from behind him.

He turned around, drawing his pistol in one fluid motion. His grip tightened, the cold steel of the trigger caressed his finger. There she was, that jade green dress draping over a perfect form.

Whisper.

"I will put a bullet through your skull faster than you can spit if you take any step toward me," She was perfectly in his sights, her left eye reflecting the still barrel in its violet iris.

"Now, now; I never brought harm to you." She smiled, sinister and macabre, sucking in his energy. Jeremiah coughed, lowering his pistol through the fit. "Well, not until now."

"Stop it! What the…" His cough grew worse, leaving Jeremiah to gasp for air. He felt as if he was drowning in an unseen ocean, "Stop!"

"Now, Jeremiah, I will stop, but you must lower your pistol and listen to the words I speak. It will be a simple request I have of you, one that anyone could fulfill."

The coughing fit ceased, his grip remained on the pistol, finger still on the trigger, yet he lowered it enough to where Whisper was barely out of the sight. He nodded, meekly, accepting her terms; well, for the time being, that is.

"Good." She said, the same calm voice she always had. He tried to figure why her voice was so collected, even after he had shot her during their first encounter. He glanced down to her leg to see no sign of a gunshot wound. "I hear this crew you're traveling with has a job, a job for someone who never pays his debts. Unfortunately, I cannot allow this to happen.

"Now, Jeremiah, we may not be on the best of terms, but I will allow you to redeem yourself. You could join my inner circle, and I would allow you a special worship." Whisper looked down at her feet, taking one hand and beginning to slowly form a circle with her finger in the air, causing a blue smoke ring to form. She looked up, seductively, and blew a kiss and a wink to Jeremiah. "Anything you would like would be yours."

Small beads of sweat began to caress Jeremiah's brow, beautiful though she was, he could never take favors from a deity that he *knew* killed Sasha, "No," he said sternly, "I'm afraid I can't help you."

"Are you sure," She took a step forward, anticipating Jeremiah to lift his pistol and fire; he didn't move, "I would accept you into my flock; feed you my wisdom, keep warm your bed, settle your mind with soothing words." She stepped forward once more, "I break no promises to those who follow my words."

Jeremiah's pistol remained lowered, his eyes fixed on Whisper's face. "Sorry, rather not." He couldn't take his eyes off her.

"I know, I know. It is all too much for a soul such as yours to grasp hold of. But you could grasp all of it; *all* of it." She continued to urge Jeremiah to follow as her fingers were forming different shapes with blue smoke before stepping forward once more to softly brush Jeremiah's cheek. "Now, kill your fake Gods, your false idols; accept me. Please, turn your back on these," She gestured a hand toward Tom and Zed, "poor fools. They will harm you, destroy that fragile soul of yours; but I can bring you into my light."

"No, I won't stand in your light; I stand in the lord's light," He stepped back, "Now, ma'am, please get off this rig."

Whisper cracked a half-smile in Jeremiah's direction, she looked over her shoulder to Zed and Tom again, letting out a sigh. "I tried to save you again, yet once more you refuse my kindness. Please, Jeremiah, be rational; don't end up a fool as the rest are." She stepped back and turned away from Jeremiah. Her shoulders and back were bare, pale, perfect. "I suppose I could spare you, maybe one day you will see my light and bask in my glory." She turned to look at Jeremiah and nodded in his direction. "I suggest you go inside."

Suddenly the rig was moving once more, Whisper had vanished; mixing her form in with the fog. Her scent lingered in the air for a brief moment, just long enough for it to touch Jeremiah's lungs for a single inhale. It smelt of fresh summer rain on the Texas prairie. Jeremiah felt weak, tired, drained of all life. He turned to the hatch, opening it and returning to the place he once sat.

He lit himself another cigarette and wondered something very serious; why had he actually returned to the safety of the rigs interior.

"Look out!" Carol called, right before the rig jolted violently and began to flip.

Jeremiah stumbled out of the smoking and rolled over rig. He was uninjured – to his knowledge – and dizzy. He didn't know how many times the rig rolled before coming to a stop, or how far they went before friction and gravity brought them to a complete stop, but he did know that he was alive.

He tried to stay on his feet, but he couldn't stay completely stable. He fell to his knees, unprepared. Stumbling forward once more he found his footing and tried to assess his situation the best he could.

Everything around him was spinning, chaotic, unusual.

He tried to wobble about the wreck, searching for any sign of life from Tom or the others. Unfortunately, Tom and Zed were nowhere to be found, more than likely they were flung off in random directions from their perches atop the rig. Carol and Jeff were still in the cab, but the impact of the crash sealed the small opening that led to their remains. He could tell by looking through the window that Carol's neck was hanging in an unnatural way, her face covered by her dark hair. Jeff was no better, as a part of the vehicle crushed onto him; his eyes remained wide open in fear.

A welling pain began to arise in his stomach; he looked down to see no wound, no blood, nothing. The pain he felt was more of a sickening sorrow, a welling, and churning in his stomach. He couldn't pinpoint who he was, what his purpose was. He fell down to his knees, partially from the unrelenting spinning, but mostly from the need for prayer.

"Father," he began, dull, slurring, "Please, please, grant me the strength to carry on. Give me the sight of what I need. Give me a path, lord, all I need is a path." He clenched his hands together, falling forward, they were the only thing separating his forehead from the dry ground. "Grant me the sight, please lord, I've lost my way."

Of course, he meant this in both the literal and spiritual sense. He no longer knew what to believe in, and he couldn't contemplate his purpose for being alive after everyone else had to perish so abruptly

The smoke from the rig filled his nose; the smell of steel soaked in fuel, burning rubber and gunpowder. He pushed the smells out of his mind before he could smell the burning, searing flesh of his companions. He reached into his satchel, but quickly recoiled; the bottle of grapefruit alcohol had shattered in the tumble. His hand began to ooze blood.

He looked inside to see the open pack of cigarettes was completely soaked, luckily the unopened ones were sealed, and he was positive those cigarettes were fine. His bible was soaked as well, along with all of his other effects. The bottle of whiskey was still in tacked, and he quickly opened it to pour a small amount on his bloody hand.

The stinging cause him to grind his teeth, clenching his jaw tightly.

He reached back into the satchel, swimming around the broken bits of glass to find the medical kit. As soon as he had hold of it, he began mending his mangled hand. As he cleaned and dressed the wound, he did his best to make sure nothing vital had been punctured.

He needed the use of that hand.

He knew he had to gather all he could carry and continue on in the direction the rig had been traveling. The rigs smoke mixed in with the fog above him as he brought himself back to his feet.

And, there he was, re-entering the overturned rig. Nothing that wasn't secured to the floor was even remotely in the same spot.; canteens of water, ammunition, scattered papers. He could only take what was useful, what he could carry. First, he grabbed some of the canteens, as well as any .22 ammunition and .44 ammunition. Unfortunately, he could only find .22 ammunition – seven rounds – that was strewn about, any of the ammunition for his Winchester was already in his satchel; only eighteen rounds. He felt helpless, lost in the Grey, no way of knowing if the direction they were heading would lead him anywhere.

As soon as he had scavenged the supplies he felt were needed, he set off in the direction the rig was traveling; Whisper's voice echoed in his head, "I suppose I could spare you…"

He felt as though he had betrayed the small crew of the rig; he should have grabbed Tom and Zed, bringing them bellow with him when his stomach began to churn. He should have figured that was Whispers way of making sure he had gone along with her plan. But why him? Why was she doing so much to interfere with his life? Why was she following him through the Grey? He had no answers, he just had the weight as he lamented over all that had happened.

CHAPTER 10

Jeremiah didn't know how far he had traveled; all he knew is the road stretched onward. He had not seen any visual markers for quite some time and began to wonder if the road really led anywhere at all. *Maybe this insane place is purgatory* he thought to himself once more before focusing his mind on the scenery – or lack thereof – around him. His eyelids were heavy, but he refused to stop without some sort of shelter, so he pressed forward with heavy steps. With the pain from the tumble and his need for sleep, he felt as if this was actually going to be the end of his time in the Grey.

The ground felt as if it began to crumble beneath his feet, crunching with each step. He stopped and looked down; a gravel road had begun at a bend he hadn't noticed to take. He looked back, seeing the road he was on connecting to the road he was now taking. Nothing surrounding the new road seemed to have any significant detail, just the same as before; nothing.

His steps became more even, slower, lighter. He wanted to make sure that if this place led somewhere unsavory he could turn tail and get out before anyone – or anything – noticed him.

His thoughts began to wander to what he called home; he could see his wife sitting on the porch as he came in from a long day tending to the cattle, Bobby playing in the dirt. That smile could light up any darkness he had, nothing more beautiful than his family being happy. That is why he avoided the war; he didn't want them to lose him, he didn't want his son to grow up with no father.

Now, he realized, he never thought what it would be like to lose both of them.

Something began to slowly push through the fog in front of him. He stopped, crouching low, squinting his eyes, trying to make sense of the structure before him. It looked rather uniformed, maybe something built after his time, yet before the Grey embraced the earth. However, he was still too far off to figure out more than the size and shape.

It was large, maybe fifteen or so feet high, and a good hundred fifty or so feet wide. It was an impressive structure, yet he could see no signs of life coming from it.

He continued his approach, slower, crouched, just in case. He didn't know whether or not he should keep his hand on his holstered pistol; he didn't know if someone was inside and if they would view him as a threat if he did. They had the higher ground, and no matter how good of a shot he was, it didn't matter if he couldn't find cover to prevent a possible rain of bullets or other projectiles the inhabitants may have.

No matter how much closer he got he could still not make out movement, no signs of life at all. He thought about calling out, but stopped himself; again, he didn't know who, or what, lingered behind the massive walls.

A chill ran up his spine as his thought went to the possibility of a demonic army within. Still, he continued forward.

As he came closer, he could begin to see the color. It looked to be a mix of brown and gray, slight hints of green. The structure was obviously built by random materials possibly scavenged from surrounding areas. He could tell some of the structure was made from finely cut wood, as well as bits of steel and tree trunks. He thought he could see the torso of a figure walking along the top, but couldn't be too sure thanks to the mist ever swirling around the land. This was most definitely a post-Grey structure.

He saw the shadow at the top again, moving from left to right. It looked like just a normal man, but Jeremiah didn't want to take any chances. He stayed where he was, crouched in the mist, watching the figure pace back and forth until he heard a voice call; "You out there! You alright?" it seemed to be coming from near the figure, but the figure just maintained its pacing. Jeremiah scanned the top of the structure, and then he saw a second figure; slim, tall, appearing to be staring straight at his position. Jeremiah knew he had been spotted, and decided it would be best to raise to his feet, hands in the air. "Woah!" the figure called out, "I didn't say surrender! Was asking if you were alright."

"Just got stuck out here," Jeremiah yelled out, making the pacing figure pause and appear to look at him, "Runnin' low on water, and some supplies. Just tryin' to find somewhere to rest."

An area of the front of the structure appeared to open slightly, "Just keep your hands up, and make your way inside. Someone's going to grab you, don't worry about it, he just wants to make sure you aren't going to be killing us or something."

Jeremiah slowly began to approach the structure. As he got closer, he could see the figures as normal men; one wearing a green, black, and brown spotted uniform, holding a rifle at ease. The other looked to be a British soldier from the revolution; read coat, single shot musket, bright gold flashy buttons. However, the rest of his uniform appeared not completely right as far as Jeremiah could tell.

With slow steps and a steady heartbeat, he finally made his way into the opening of the structure where he was indeed apprehended by a strong hand on his back. He kept his hands up as the man searched his pockets, and checked his weapons.

"All good!" the man called up to the others on the wall, "He has weapons, but not much else. Want me to take them?"

"No," The other man called down, "He tries anything, I'm pretty sure we got him outnumbered fairly well."

"Welcome to the outpost," the man who had checked Jeremiah said before disappearing into a small door at the wall.

Jeremiah found himself in a small makeshift building in the middle of the massive walls. Around him were rounds of ammunition, and weapons, as well as canned goods and other essentials. He searched, trying to find the proper ammunition for his rifle and pistol among the piles of boxes and bags. Once a few extra rounds were located he tried to find anything else he could find a use for but to no avail. He paid for the ammunition and exited the small shop.

There were many makeshift buildings, all placed throughout the walls in an organized manner. No side seemed too cluttered or chaotic, and if it weren't for the random building materials one could say that the outpost was made before the Grey had struck. Some of the structures were obviously small homes, while others appeared to be miscellaneous businesses. After scanning for a short while he saw one that he assumed was the building he'd hoped there would be; a saloon.

The saloon looked to be two stories, possibly a bar on one story and some rooms for rent on the other. He knew he should find a place to rest his weary head, yet the call of a stiff drink that didn't come from his own bottle could be exactly what he needed before he turned tail and returned to wandering; only this time he would wander alone.

He made his way through a tall door, barely sealed around the sides, it's hinges allowing it to scrape across the floor as he swung it open. There were few patrons sitting at the scattered tables in the bar, and none of them turned to see who was coming in; they seemed to be too preoccupied with conversation and drinks. One man sat – or more laid – at a piano that had obviously come into disuse and disrepair. The tables, on the other hand, looked new and barely used. He found himself the closest table and sat down. He noticed a charred wooden bowl planted at the center of the table, half smoked cigarettes plastered upright in their own ashes within the bowls curve.

He fished in his jacket for a fresh cigarette. As he pushed it up to his lips and lit it, a young woman made her way over to his table.

"What'll it be, sweetie?" She asked as she stopped at the side of his table. She wore a dark blue skirt, hiding high heels of the same color, and a sea foam green top; the combo contoured her body in all the right ways. She looked to be in her mid to late twenties, with long black hair, and eyes the color of the deepest oceans. Her smile was intoxicating, and her voice was soothing and well mannered. He tried to place her accent, yet could not as his tired mind trailed to what would be good to drink.

"Whiskey." He replied, with a gravely low voice. His decision took longer than it should have, but he was in no position to think properly.

"Aw," she said, "You just here for the whiskey, or conversation?" Her voice had a smile in it; genuine, not just something to keep up appearances at work.

To be honest, he did want the conversation, but he knew he couldn't hold one with a woman who looked at him in that way. To him, it brought up memories of the first time he met his late wife.

"I'll have a whiskey," Was all he could say as he took another drag from his cigarette.

She sighed, and wandered to the back, disappearing behind a small set of double doors. Jeremiah sat there, looking down at the new table varnish. He wouldn't have been able to tell if another man had ever sat at this table if it weren't for the cigarettes and ash. That thought comforted him in some peculiar way, as it meant others enjoyed the company of whiskey and a cigarette.

A short moment of thought passed before she returned with a glass of whiskey and placed it in front of him. He looked up, trying to grace her with a smile, but was unable to before she slowly began walking away; glancing back to him every so often. Jeremiah savored the whiskey, feeling it burn down his esophagus, and into his mostly empty stomach. The feeling was, unfortunately, hollow, as if his body missed the memo of fresh alcohol.

His eyes wandered about the room; from face to face, stool to chair, glass to glass. The saloon was very basic, only about ten small tables, as well as a bar toward the back of the building where the young woman had disappeared to get Jeremiah his drink. The place smelled of stale cigar smoke and old rain, a hint of sweat hidden beneath.

It was obvious the bar had good use made of it from the scuffed and dinged floors, as well as the dirty glasses in which drinks were served. Still, it was something he had expected from the outpost; he was sure they had their share of couriers coming through looking for a bed as well as a drink. He admired the craftsmanship of the table, running his fingers across its smooth metallic finish, wondering how many drinks it had seen.

The door scraped along the floor as someone entered the bar. Jeremiah sat still, sipping on his drink as he heard heavy footsteps approaching him from behind. He contemplated who had entered the bar as he saw two men sitting at a table look up at the figure coming up behind him. From the footsteps, Jeremiah could detect an ever so slight limp, yet wasn't able to presume much more before a hand met his shoulder. Instinctually he placed a hand on his pistol, ready to draw it.

"Settle down there," a man's voice said with authority. "Just knew you came into the fort, was told about your firearms."

The man eventually made his way into Jeremiah's view, and took a seat across from him at the table. He wore a civil war uniform; blue, decorated with the markings of a general. His blonde mustache hung low, below his chin, his hair pristinely cut and groomed, both showing hints of age with graying whiskers here and there. His eyes were hardened by combat, yet through their gray, he could see glints of hope and care.

"How's it goin', Billy Yank?" Jeremiah said between sips of his whiskey, his eyes darting between the table, the man, and the glass.

"Not all too good, Johnny Reb." He replied before coughing. He revealed a small off-white handkerchief that was tucked into his belt. The handkerchief was speckled with brown and red and was tattered through much use.

"No," Jeremiah said, shaking his head as he pulled a cigarette out of his jacket, "Just a Texan, I didn't fight no war."

"Well, do you have a name, 'just a Texan'?"

"You first," Jeremiah replied, cigarette hanging from the left corner of his mouth. His eyes were fixed on the man as he pulled out a match to light the cigarette

"Names Chamberlain" He extended his hand for Jeremiah to shake, "General Chamberlain."

"Washington" he replied, lighting his cigarette, ignoring Chamberlain's hand. He wasn't sure why he had used his proper last name as his introduction, but something inside of him told him to. "Jus' call me Wash. Can I help you?"

Smoke began to billow out of his mouth, encompassing his straw hair. He looked down at his glass, taking another sip. He was too tired to deal with whatever Chamberlain wanted, and he knew there was about to be some sort of proposal.

"Well, Wash," Chamberlain began, "I've been collecting fighters. Nothing serious, just trying to give people a sense of normalcy around here. Already rounded up close to eighteen. Trying to get this town secure, as well as the surrounding area."

"I'm the wrong guy to be talkin' to," He took a long drag from the cigarette, looking Chamberlain in the eye as the smoke exited his mouth and filled the air.

The General just looked at him, those hardened eyes studying the details in Jeremiah's face. Jeremiah wondered what was running through his mind; how he thought Jeremiah could help, what he *needed* Jeremiah for, or even where the hell these surrounding towns may be.

Chamberlain called over the waitress and waited a moment for her to reach their table. "Give this man whatever drinks he orders tonight, put them on the military tab, would you please, Alexis?"

She nodded, and disappeared into the back room, only to re-emerge holding a glass of whiskey and a pint of ale. She set the ale in front of Chamberlain, and the whiskey in front of Jeremiah just as he put his empty glass down from his lips. She winked at Jeremiah as she took his empty glass, but he ignored her again.

"Thank you for the generosity, General, but I can't help much. Haven't really had the best-a-luck in my travels so far, and I'm not thinkin' I'd be much help here."

"Got a wife?" Chamberlain asked, watching the waitress walk away.

"The hell did you ask?" Jeremiah snapped, rage and sadness dancing within his eyes. He felt the pain all over again, replaying his first day in this God forsaken land. He should've stayed home, dug himself a hole, and taken his own life then.

"Sorry, didn't mean to offend you. It's just," Chamberlain gestured his raised glass to Alexis behind the counter of the bar. Jeremiah didn't turn, but he knew exactly where he was pointing as if he could see her figure without thought. "pretty young woman like that makes eyes at you, and you aren't even interested." He sipped his beer, "Where is she?"

Jeremiah didn't know how to respond, he downed the whiskey, slamming the empty glass onto the table with such force the shock went through his hand, up his arm, and infected his skull. The chatter from other patrons in the bar went silent for a moment before resuming.

Jeremiah leaned forward over the table, lookin at Chamberlain as if the room had vanished around them, "Rather not talk about it." Tears slowly began to make their way into his eyes, being held back by an invisible dam. The room went blurry, but he could make out the outline of Alexis bringing a fresh glass of whiskey to the table.

"My condolences," Chamberlain said, in a soft understanding voice.

Jeremiah settled back in his chair, slouching as his hand found the fresh glass of whiskey. He wiped his eyes clear with the back of his other hand and noticed Alexis still standing at the table. She was looking down at Jeremiah, an apologetic and concerned smile embedded in her face; her eyes steady, wide with apology as if she knew exactly what their conversation had been about. She turned away slowly and made her way over to another table.

"How about this, enjoy your drinks tonight, and you can stay in one of the barracks. Tomorrow I can help you find a job in this town, no matter what that may be." Chamberlain sipped his ale, looking around the room, he leaned in close to Jeremiah, "Just think about it."

"Thank you," Jeremiah replied with a shaky voice as he watched Chamberlain finish off his ale.

Chamberlain extended his hand to Jeremiah. This time, Jeremiah did the same, feeling a firm handshake from callus palms before he made his way out of the bar, leaving Jeremiah alone in his seat with ash hanging off his cigarette and a whiskey that was slowly going warm in his hand. He took another sip and then extinguished his cigarette completely on the table itself; *A scar, from me to you. Some character*, he thought to himself.

CHAPTER 11

The bunks in the barracks were firm, yet it was probably the softest mattress he had felt in a long time. He couldn't tell the time of day, nor how long he had laid there before sleep finally consumed his soul.

It wasn't really sleeping, more an intoxicated coma that honestly did nothing to rejuvenate his body or mind from the aches and chaotic thoughts. Yet, he had no choice when it came to waking up; it was the sound of commotion and people screaming that finally made him stir.

"Attack incoming!" A man's voice called from somewhere, cracking into Jeremiah's skull, reverberating behind his eyes, "Get up! Get out! HOLD THE LINE! We have to defend what we've worked so hard to build; get a move on!"

Jeremiah rolled out of his bunk, crashing hard against the cold steel floor. He took a moment, on his hands and knees, trying to remember his surroundings. Everything was blurry, spinning around him, causing him to heave up bile onto the floor. The smell penetrated his nostrils, causing him to gag and heave again, yet his stomach turned up nothing from his plea to expel whatever may have been left. He looked around, noticing his rifle leaned up against the wall off to his left. He made his way, stumbling and falling the entire way, eventually coming within arm's reach of his Winchester.

He reached out, knocking the rifle onto the ground. It came down with a clank as the steel and wood met with the floor. He scrambled to it, pulling it from where it fell, and inspected it quickly to make sure he hadn't knocked it too hard on the ground. The rifle was in perfect working order, yet he realized there was no ammunition. He scanned the room which was still spinning, trying to locate his satchel. It wasn't hanging from his bunk, nor was it on the floor, he couldn't seem to locate it anywhere. He closed his eyes, trying to remember where it may have been from the night before, but the commotion coming from around the barracks made it hard to concentrate.

He lifted himself from the floor and made his way to the door. From the corner of his eye he saw his satchel; hunched up against the corner of the room with his jacket covering it just enough to where he couldn't see it from his earlier vantage point. He rushed over, frantically emptying the contents onto the floor. He gathered some of the ammunition, filling the tumbler magazine to its maximum capacity before grabbing a handful of rounds and shoving them in his pocket as he made his way out the door.

Although the fog and light were the exact same as when he had entered the barracks, it stung his eyes, forcing him to blink several times before he could see the chaos of fifteen or so men running up and down the stairs of the surrounding wall. He made his way as quickly as possible up the steps, avoiding others who quickly passed him in both directions. He could hear yelling, screaming; directions, strategy, ammunition needed. Finally, he was on top of the wall, looking out into the mist. He couldn't see any enemy approaching, yet he could hear sounds from all around the area surrounding the fort; calling from the mist, mocking him.

Finally, he caught a glimpse of movement off to his right. He ran to a position on the wall, joined by three other soldiers. They all steadied their rifles against the wall, peering off into the distance, waiting for the approaching invasion. The shadows moved chaotically about as if trying to distract them. Jeremiah recalled tales of the Natives attacking forts and outposts that his father had told him. How the Natives would distract the guns by causing a diversion away from the approaching force, catching the soldiers and settlers by surprise when the actual attack came from the side or rear. He saw the shadows of the distant figures dancing, running side to side, flashing small lights to the fort; this was a distraction.

He pulled his rifle from the wall and stood up, scanning the surrounding area. Other soldiers on the wall were searching for the invasion as well. His eyesight kept blurring and trying to focus thanks to the unfortunate hangover from the whiskey. He tried to regain his concentration, but every sound cluttered his mind. Finally, off in the distance to the rear of the fort, he saw movement. He ran, keeping his balance on the walkway, he knew he had to make it over there before they began to charge.

Luckily, when he reached the rear, he was greeted by Chamberlain and seven soldiers. The soldiers were already set up, aiming at the approaching mass, waiting to open fire. Jeremiah settled himself within the ranks, putting his rifle against the wall to steady his aim. He squinted, looking down the sight of his rifle, ready to defend the wall at all costs; *Nothin' to lose anyway*, he thought as he saw a small flame fly from the approaching army. It exploded with a clank against the wall, spewing flames up past the men's rifles, yet leaving them unfazed and unharmed.

Another fireball whizzed to the wall, causing the same effect. Jeremiah could feel the heat crash against his face.

"Open fire!" Chamberlain called out from behind.

BANG! Click.

Jeremiah took his first shot; watching his target fall in a spurt of blood. He could hear shouts from the others in his sights; cursing and sputtering in an unknown and ancient language. He steadied his aim once more, finding his next target. He saw a man lighting a cloth in a bottle, the flame illuminating his scarred and ragged face. The man cocked the bottle with one arm behind him.

BANG! Click.

Blood erupted from a hole in the man's neck. He fell backward onto the lit bottle, causing flames to burst in all directions from under his body. Two others were caught by the flame before bullets from Chamberlain's men brought them down.

The chaos of the battle was in full swing as Jeremiah tried to find his next target. Men were falling on the battlefield, yet no bullets were being fired in their direction; just bottles of combustible liquid and spears.

BANG! Click.

The third bullet caught one of the invaders in the shoulder, causing him to stumble before continuing his approach.

BANG! Click.

The man fell forward as Jeremiah's fourth bullet hit him perfectly in the heart, spraying blood out his back in a plume of red that mixed with the surrounding fog. Still, the approach of the others continued. Jeremiah tried to count the approaching force as quickly as possible before taking his next shot; thirty.

BANG! Click.

Twenty-nine. Twenty-eight. Twenty-seven. Chamberlain's men knew what they were doing, amazing accuracy, great composure. Jeremiah looked around at the men to his sides; they were well composed, eyes on the targets. Just then, a spear flew up and caught one of the men in the chest. His eyes widened before he fell backward, off the wall and onto a building below with a dull thud. None of the soldiers batted an eye. He saw chamberlain, shooting a pistol into the oncoming army, his face a stone, not even blinking.

Just then, something came over Jeremiah. His vision tunneled, all sound escaped the air; it was just him, his heartbeat, his breath, his bullets, his targets.

BANG! Click.

His bullet found a young man right in-between the eyes. Then, it all went black as he remembered his son's face as the bullet met with his flesh, Jeremiah felt the warm hollow barrel of his rifle press against his chin. A vision of his son flashed before his eyes.

"Papa, don't. Papa, wake up, I'm here…"

Suddenly Jeremiah was brought back to reality as his rifle was jerked from his hands, knocking his head back as it cracked against his jaw. He opened his eyes to be greeted by Chamberlains' face, concern crossed his brow as he looked at Jeremiah. His men were behind him, horror plaster on their faces. Chamberlain was holding the Winchester in his hand.

"I'd rather keep your shot," Chamberlain said, holding the Winchester out for Jeremiah. "Don't do something stupid like that again."

Jeremiah turned, looking out onto the battlefield. The enemy had fallen, not a single survivor among them. He turned back to Chamberlain's men who were still staring in shock. He tried to place the confused and horrified look on their face, trying to figure out what had happened, but he couldn't. Chamberlain was still holding out the Winchester, still waiting for Jeremiah to take it. He didn't know how to react, but Chamberlain pressed the rifle into his chest. Jeremiah clenched onto the rifle with both arms.

"Like I said, I'd rather keep your shot. Now, if you have some demons in your head that might jeopardize the safety of my troops or this town, I suggest you take care of them as soon as possible. Until then, I don't want to see you on the line unless I call for you; are we clear?"

"Yes, sir," Jeremiah replied, straightening himself out. He gave a weak salute before Chamberlain turned and walked down the stairs and out of sight.

Jeremiah returned to his bunk, tired and covered in sweat. He cleaned up his belongings that were scattered about the floor from his quick scramble to find ammunition. He retrieved lose cigarettes and bullets, as well as gold pieces that were scattered about. Lighting one of the cigarettes, he put the rest of his effects back where they belonged.

His hangover was still there, discomfort bouncing between his stomach and head as he planted himself on the edge of his bunk. He began to inspect and clean his rifle, cigarette smoke stinging his eyes as he took it apart, carefully examining each part before placing them next to him. Everything seemed to be in good working order, albeit a bit dirty with use and lack of maintenance.

It was quiet in the room. Although it had enough bunks to sleep eight men, he was the only one who resided in this particular barrack for the time being. The space was large and cold thanks to the predominantly steel structure receiving no sunlight in the fog. Jeremiah knew that eventually, the room would have other soldiers in it, but until then he enjoyed the solitude. He continued his task before he was interrupted by a knock at the door.

"Come in." He said, not looking up from his partially disassembled rifle. He heard the door open, and footsteps approach him. The steps were light, slight clicks, not at all like the heavy footsteps of a soldier. He looked up to see Alexis holding a clear canteen of water before returning to his task at hand.

"Thank you for helping defend the town." She said, her voice still just as sweet and smooth as it had been the night before. "Chamberlain said you might need some water, so I volunteered to bring it to you."

She crouched a moment, just long enough to put the water at his feet before she straightened her posture. She held her hands together loosely in front of her, studying Jeremiah for just a moment before she began to turn and walk away. She relaxed her face once Jeremiah could no longer see it, a sigh almost escaped her lips before Jeremiah spoke, stopping her short of the door.

"You didn't have to, ma'am," He was still looking down at his rifle, disassembling it with the cigarette hanging out of his mouth, "Honest, I woulda been just fine."

She turned to face him, noticing a half smile cracking his lips as he took the cigarette out of his mouth. He held the cigarette between his pointer and middle finger as he flicked the butt with his thumb, watching the ash float down to the floor before returning it to his mouth. "No, sweetie, it was honestly my pleasure. If you need anything at all, you know where to find me."

"Thank you." He said, looking up at her, giving her a wide smile, "Good to know there's still some good around here."

Alexis exited the building, waiting to smile until the door was completely closed behind her. She began to blush, as she hurried her way back to the saloon. Her heart was fluttering the entire walk to the doors. She took a moment to regain her composure before going inside and making her way up to her room. She felt like a schoolgirl; for the first time in a long time, she felt like something better was in this world.

Four cigarettes, that is how long it took for Jeremiah to finish disassembling, cleaning, and then reassembling his beloved Winchester. Four cigarettes of pure thoughtless muscle memory. But, his life was far from thoughtless actions, and that became evidentially clear as his hand placed the final piece of the rifle back together; the forend. He ran his finger over the carving he put there from so many days before. Unlike the last time, no tears came to his eyes as he read each letter, but his soul felt a hole tearing larger.

It was a pain unseen, yet so very real to him.

He finished the last cigarette and collected the other three cigarette butts from the floor. Opening the door, he placed them outside on the dirt ground to the right. He took a deep breath of the air, exhaling only once his lungs couldn't hold any more air.

Texas air.

He closed the door and walked back over to his bunk. He saw the water that Alexis had placed for him still sitting untouched on the floor. He smiled as he picked it up and took a sip, *some good still in this world.*

CHAPTER 12

Chamberlain was a man of honor, as well as a man forged in the brutal conflict of war; yet – like many others who fell into the Grey – he never thought this was where his life was heading. He rubbed his naked right foot as it touched the rough cold floor. Although the battle before was routine, it left him rattled from what he had seen. Applying weight to his foot was not favored as he began to stand from his small sweat soaked bed. He shifted his weight from his right foot to his left as he hobbled his way over to a small table that was right under an open window.

He pulled open a rickety drawer and retrieved a small clear bottle. He tilted it into his hand to retrieve a small pill labeled *Vicodin*. He hated the fact that his hip and foot forced him to resort to a pill in order to function and command his men. He usually would refuse to take them, but today it was almost a necessity.

He threw the small pill into his mouth, chasing it with water as he looked out the window. Some of his men were patrolling the walls, getting ready for the next patrol to take their position so that they could retire to their quarters.

He turned away from his window and walked, as best he could, over to his bed. He pulled his boots out from under his bed and began to shine them. It was funny how something he had done day in and day out for his entire adult life brought him a sense of comfort in the Grey.

As soon as the mundane calming task was finished, he grabbed his uniform that hung on the wall next to his bed. Its buttons were a glittering gold, connected golden yellow insignias and designs. The blue in the uniform had faded slightly after years of wear, but it was still distinguishable from the other uniforms his soldiers who fell through from other eras had sported.

He took a moment to dress, and then combed his hair and waxed his mustache. Afterwards he made his way over to the door. The *Vicodin* had only just begun to kick in at this point, so his limp was less defined, yet still apparent. He opened the door and saw one of his soldiers, Private Robinson, posted at attention for guard detail. He was dressed in his era uniform; Olive drab, with tan bags and belt, brown boots that extended up to his knee. He was a good soldier, well-mannered and proper. Even when he was off duty and in his "civilian" attire, he would still snap to attention and salute when his superiors would pass by. Once Chamberlain exited his quarters, Private Robinson saluted rigidly while not moving his eyes.

"At ease," Chamberlain said. He did appreciate how the Private was so focused on his duty and respect, but this was no longer a real army, as much as he wanted it to be. "You know that your detail ended about an hour ago. I don't mind you taking your leave."

"Sir, current circumstances require me to stand guard. We don't know if another attack is incoming. Just trying to make sure you are safe, sir." He did another quick salute.

"Alright, well, go grab yourself something to eat, I'm about to do the same." Chamberlain began to walk away, yet a few paces away he realized that Robinson was still posted at his door. "Come on now, breakfast should be ready any moment," Chamberlain called back to the soldier.

Robinson began to march forward, taking up position next to Chamberlain. Chamberlain gave him a tap on the shoulder, and finally, Robinson began to walk in a normal manner, no longer acting as if he were on duty. His shoulders slouched forward a bit, and his steps became less on tempo.

"How did the stranger do it?" Robinson said, "He should've been done in, but instead he's still walking about like nothing happened. Almost taking a slug straight to the bean? That just isn't right. What do you think? Magic? A God? Demon?"

"No idea," Chamberlain replied, furrowing his brow, "He sure as hell isn't possessed. It's just something new and strange in the Grey. Who knows, maybe it's a ghost from the past haunting his battle ground."

Jeremiah awoke after a short nap. The smell of cigarettes had already subsided, and the stale air returned to normal. He sat up, cracking his neck side to side. He reached for a cigarette, lighting it as he rose from the bed. He scratched his chin as he took his first puff, contemplating what would happen to him. His mind wandered from leaving the small secluded fort, all the way to how many people that he had encountered were in favor of a new god.

He paced the floors, barefoot, feeling his feet press against the cold steel. His stomach growled, unappeased by the small canteen of water he had finished before he fell back into the sweet sleep he had needed. He knew he needed something to eat, so, with a lit cigarette, he began to lace up his boots.

Once he gathered his belongings, he opened the door and

stepped outside. The morning – or was it the afternoon – air slapped his face, rejuvenating.

He made his way, step by step, to the saloon he had drank at the night before. He figured with the buildings scattered about, that would be a reasonable place to get a hot meal. Nothing else in the area looked like a restaurant; there was a store, three barracks, maybe eight to ten houses, and the saloon. He was sure there had to be somewhere that the troops ate together, but he couldn't determine where that may be. As he walked, he could feel the eyes of those around him pierce into his spirit. Something was amiss from the night before, and he couldn't determine why his mind had decided that in the heat of battle was the best place to reunite with his departed family.

Possibly – probably – it was the image of the young attacker taking the rushing lead through his head.

He finally reached the saloon, pushing open the door. As soon as his foot touched the floor, he could smell eggs and sausage cooking. He closed his eyes, taking in a deep breath, savoring the scent as if it were the first time he'd smelled it. He opened his eyes and made his way to an empty table before a familiar face caught his eye.

Chamberlain was sitting with another soldier, beckoning Jeremiah to join them with one hand as he put a tin mug of coffee to his mouth with the other. The soldier looked up and behind, looking for whoever Chamberlain was waving for. When his eyes fell onto Jeremiah, they grew wide with some unknown horror for a brief moment before he turned back to his breakfast.

Jeremiah made his way over, taking a seat next to the unknown soldier. The soldier extended a hand to Jeremiah, "Private Robinson," he said, waiting for Jeremiah to accept his hand. As soon as Jeremiah extended his own in a firm handshake he continued, "You must be Wash. You did a number earlier. Thought you might've been punch-drunk, but it worked!"

Jeremiah had no way of figuring out a response, he just nodded and turned to Chamberlain who was still sipping on his coffee. Chamberlain looked just as he did last night, in his blue and gold uniform, mustache and hair pristine. He looked at Jeremiah, lowering the mug from his mouth "Hungry?" Chamberlain said.

"Yes, sir," Jeremiah replied, scooting the seat closer to the table. "What's to eat?"

Alexis walked over to the table, catching Jeremiah's eye. She looked down to hide her smile, but he could still see it. She was holding a clear pot of coffee in one hand, her other hand perched on her hip. "Egg's alright?" She said as she reached the table, "Would offer a side of bacon, but we're fresh out."

"Egg's sounds fine." Jeremiah said, "Do you happen to have some tea?"

"Of course," she said to Jeremiah before turning to Chamberlain, "Your food will be out in a moment, need a refill?"

She held the coffee pot up as Chamberlain held out his glass. She turned to Robinson who waved her off as he took a sip out of his own mug. She turned away and walked to the doors located behind the bar. Jeremiah watching her walking away, he did his best to hide it but felt as if everyone knew he was studying her walk.

He turned his attention back to the two men who were busy sipping at their coffee and chatting to have noticed his brief thought of Alexis. "So, Chamberlain," He said, interrupting whatever topic they happened to be on, "I've had a bit of a chance to think."

Chamberlain looked over at Jeremiah, his brow furrowed in question and surprise as the coffee pressed against his lips. He took a sip before returning his mug to the table, "Thinking?" He said, "What did you think about."

"About your offer, to stay here."

"Hmm…" Chamberlain replied, smoothing his mustache, "Well, I know you have a good shot, a damn good shot. The only problem is; you have some demons to deal with. Now, I'd love to have you among the ranks, but you need to keep that head on straight."

"Agreed" Robinson chimed in, his mug pressing against his lower lip.

Jeremiah opened his mouth, but before he could speak he was interrupted by Alexis bringing two plates of eggs and bacon over. She placed one in front of Chamberlain, and the other in front of Robinson.

She pulled her hair back from her face and around her ear, "I'll have your tea right out in a second, sweetie," Alexis said to Jeremiah before turning away from the table. He watched as she walked over to another table close to the bar, talking to the patrons who were finishing up their meal for a moment before she disappeared from sight behind the doors.

Jeremiah turned his attention back to the two men. "The point is, General," Jeremiah said as the two began to eat their breakfast, "I can help a bit, at least before I have to move on." The truth is, Jeremiah became accustomed to having no real reason to stay anywhere since he had left his former home.

"Move on?" Robinson queried through a mouthful of eggs, covering his mouth with his hand.

"Never mind," Jeremiah replied. He didn't want to explain his situation to anyone in the town. He had already revealed his face too much to Chamberlain on the night he arrived, and he wished he hadn't. "Just know, I can help in some way. Let me know what you need, and I-"

Alexis came over and placed a plate of eggs as well as a mug of hot tea in front of Jeremiah. "Thank you." He said, looking up to catch her smile.

"Now," Chamberlain said, "As I said, I want to keep your shot. However, I'd rather not have you in that situation again. As a commander, I want my troops alive, well, and stable. So, what could I do with a man who isn't able to keep it all together in a battle?"

Jeremiah stopped himself mid-sip of his tea, he wanted to yell, scream at Chamberlain that he could take anything thrown at him. "Well, sir, I don't know what happened." Is all that came out of his mouth in as calm a manner as possible.

"Sir, what if we have him train?" Robinson had a slight quake and squeak in his voice, "You said it yourself, he has a good shot. Or we could have him help run supplies."

"Run supplies?"

"Now," Chamberlain was smoothing his mustache again before leaning in close on the table, "That wouldn't be a bad idea. Wash. You got a hell of a shot, and you wandered here on your own. Maybe you could handle both, and you'd be able to fight still as needed." He looked at Jeremiah, trying to study his facial expression, "Think you'd be capable?"

Jeremiah contemplated the idea to himself, running a finger around the rim of his mug. It could be easy, something that could pass the time until he was able to find a way out of here. But, at the same time, it could make him want to stay longer, it could make him find feelings for the people in this town. If there was one thing Jeremiah had learned from his brief time in the Grey, it was that you shouldn't get too attached to those around you.

Finally, he came to the answer. Lifting his cup up slightly above his head, he looked at Chamberlain, "You got a deal, General." He sipped his tea not breaking eye contact with Chamberlain.

"Good," Chamberlain said as he returned to his eggs.

Alexis sat in her room above the bar, looking out the window as she drank a tall glass of tea with ice floating up to the brim. It felt good to sit down after a long night leading to an early morning. She was tired, yet she felt like she had enough energy to take on the world. Something new was in the air, even in the Grey she could tell something was different in the little fort.

She watched the soldiers patrolling the wall, as some of the citizens walked from the store to their homes. There weren't many non-soldiers in the fort, maybe only fifteen or sixteen including herself, but those numbers were much lower only about a year ago (if you were able put a time on the never-ending twilight). She was one of the original civilians in this town, back before the wall was completed and Chamberlain was only a name she knew from high school history class. Back then the only buildings were three homes and the store; a simple one-meter-high dirt and stone wall surrounding it.

When she fell through, she got lucky – if you could call it lucky – according to the four people who originally inhabited the town. She was walking to work one night after a class at her community college. When the Grey completely consumed her, it left her standing only a few feet from the small dirt wall, and someone in the town was instantly there to calm her. From there, it was all downhill for a short while. Raids happened, buildings burned, liars and thieves sauntered in, people came and went, yet she remained as it was all she knew in the strange place.

Thankfully, Chamberlain came along with three other soldiers only two months after she fell through. As soon as he arrived, he regained order, assigned jobs. He was able to have the massive wall built within a few short weeks.

After the wall was built no raids were able to get to the inhabitants inside. Life in the town seemed to be almost normal, increasing morale and productivity. The only exception was the fact that there were no creature comforts she was familiar with from the twentieth century. All in all, however, she felt comfortable and safe.

The saloon was a somewhat new addition to the town, having been built around the same time as the three massive barracks. Before she worked there, she would help maintain the buildings as well as collect debris from just outside the wall for whatever reason the citizens needed them.

It wasn't terrible, it just wasn't what she was used to as work.

Since high school she had worked at the local *Denny's*, waitressing there for so long that she had seen more employees come and go than she could remember. It took her quite some time to realize she wanted more out of life than those damn managers could understand, so she started college on her 24th birthday. For her, it was slow going; taking one or two classes each semester, staying up late to study as well as work, all while trying to pay rent in a dinky one-bedroom apartment that always seemed to need something fixed every week.

No, in a way the Grey was a blessing even if everyone else felt otherwise. She loved her small room above the saloon; it may have been smaller than the one she left behind, but it felt more like home.

Her walls were covered with paintings she had made, as well as trinkets she found and traded for. Her dresser was full of clothing she could only have dreamed of back before she fell through; gowns that flowed in the wind, form fitting pants that actually felt reasonable against her skin. She enjoyed the fact that she could dress however she wanted and no one turned an eye or reprimanded her.

The Grey was something that set her free in a sense.

She wandered from her window over to her bed. It was larger than the bed she had in her old apartment, but not the *California King* she had always wanted. She put her half empty glass of tea on a small bedside table before she flopped down onto the sweet soft bedding. She looked up at the ceiling; support beams exposed, holding up the tin roofing at a slight angle. Slowly, her eyes began to close, beckoning her mind to the sweet solace of sleep. She sighed, rolling onto her side, her long blue dress tangling her legs together. She felt a smile purse her lips as her consciousness escaped her.

It was time to dream, dream about the lonesome stranger who entered her world.

CHAPTER 13

Jeremiah stood before three soldiers, young men who seemed to have never known the brutality of combat. They had rifles of different time periods slung over their shoulders, ammunition at their feet. They all stood at attention, one hand pinned to the side, the other holding the butts of rifles. He studied them, looking at their still eyes and freshly shined boots.

Soldiers, that they were, but they were unskilled. Chamberlain gave him a job; teach these boys how to shoot.

"Alright," He said to the three fresh faces, their composure remaining unhindered by his voice, "So, looks like I gotta teach y'all to shoot. Well, I'm no military man, so I don't know what you're used to, but I'll be damned if I can't get you to pick your target each time," He paused, pacing from soldier to soldier with his hands behind his back, "We'll start with me seeing what you can do. Follow me."

Jeremiah took the lead as the soldiers fell in behind him after gathering their ammunition. They followed him, making their way over to the exit of the wall, single file in perfect step. Jeremiah walked normally, looking out of place among the troops. Although he may not have been officially trained in the art of combat, he had learned the skills needed not only from his time in the Grey but also from his father.

He thought back to the time when he was only about ten; his father had ridden in with a new rifle slung over his shoulder. That was Jeremiah's rifle, his first rifle, and his father taught him to shoot it for hours every day after his chores and studying were finished. Those were good times, good days; days he wanted to share with Bobby.

He never got that chance.

His silent thoughts and the short march were interrupted by the soldier in the back. "No offense, but why in the red Hell are *you* training us. *You* aren't even a fucking soldier, let alone a commander."

Jeremiah halted, the soldiers stumbling to not bump into each other as they quickly stopped in their tracks. He spun around on his heel to face the soldiers; the man in the back poking his head out from the side to make sure Jeremiah saw the look plastered on his face. It was the kind of look you would give to a child when they were being condescending to their elders.

That look didn't settle well with Jeremiah.

"What the Hell did *you* say?" Jeremiah said, walking to the man in the back of the line.

Yes, he wasn't even a soldier in Jeremiahs eyes; soldiers had respect to those who were training them. He looked the man up and down; his blue uniform covered in small squares and rectangles of black and white. On his left breast bore a small patch with *U.S. Navy* embroidered in light blue, his right a nametag reading *Madock*.

"I said, *why* ar-"

"No, no. This is how it is. I'm gonna to teach you to shoot, you're going to report back to Chamberlain, and then I'm going to have a drink tonight. Now, if you decide to undermine me one more *fucking* time, I will make damn sure you are practicing your shot while I sip my whiskey and still will be able to outshoot you. Got it?" By the end of his rant, he was yelling only an inch away from the Madock's face. The man cowered slightly, flinching as one sentence ended and the other began.

Once Jeremiah had finished, Madock – the man - looked him dead in the eye, "Yes, *sir*."

Jeremiah could hear the sarcastic tone in his voice, yet ignored it as he walked back to the front of the soldiers, continuing to lead them to the outside of the wall. Once they had reached their destination, he halted the troops and walked forty paces away from the wall. He took four empty tin cans from his satchel and placed them on a small mound on the ground. Once he figured they were a good distance from one another, he made his way back to the troops.

"Alright, from left to right, fire at the can in front of you. You have five shots; after that, you hold your fire. Understood?"

"Yes, sir!" The two soldiers and the man barked in unison.

The first soldier stepped forward. He wore a wide-brimmed hat much like Jeremiah's, however, one side of the brim was pinned up to the crown, a strap clutched tightly to his chin. He wore a long sleeve tan button down, a pocket on each breast, sleeves rolled up to just above the elbow. Shorts with the same color came to just above the knee, brown ankle high boots with long knee high socks. He saw no distinguishing markings, yet he bore a small tin nametag reading *Martin*. The name tag looked to be handmade, almost new as if he had been given it after arriving at the fort.

Martin took aim and fired off five rounds in very quick succession, his trigger finger a blur. The rounds popped off, flying towards their target, but hitting the ground behind, causing plumes of dust and debris to fly off into the air. Five shots, the can stood unscathed, glinting the reflection of scattered light. Martin mechanically slung his rifle over his shoulder and marched back into the ranks.

The second soldier hesitated a moment before taking his place at the firing line. His stance tactical, pulling his rifle up. His uniform was all gray, plates of black emphasized his physique, black boots hidden under long gray pants. A helmet with sharp corners was on his head, a triangle ranking was embedded into the back with the name *Larcow* inside. He took a moment, taking aim at the small target. He concentrated before releasing his five rounds from the barrel of his rifle to the target down range. The bullets had a green trail from the rifle to their final resting place. Again, nothing but the ground met with the bullets. However, his shots were all just slightly low, missing his can by a few inches at most.

The final man – not soldier – Madock stepped up before Larcow had even lowered his weapon. He positioned his rifle at the ready, and without thinking, he fired off in the general direction of the can. Jeremiah couldn't even see the clouds of dust from where the bullets landed, but he also never heard a *clink* of the can being hit. No, there was no sign of the bullets at all. Madock sighed and stepped back in line with the others.

"Alright," Jeremiah let out a long exhale, forcing his lips to flap. "I see… Let me show ya how I shoot, then we'll figure out how to get your shots better."

He stepped out in front of the men, easing his rifle into position. His sight tunneled, blurring on the edges, keeping the can in view. His finger flinched as it approached the trigger. He exhaled slowly as he squeezed the trigger in-between heartbeats. The first bullet met perfectly with the tin can, causing it to fly off the small mound and roll away.

The following three cans all followed suit with the next three shots. He stopped; one single bullet still in the chamber. He looked back at the troops; two of them were standing, mouths agape in shock. With his lever action rifle, he eliminated all the targets within five seconds.

Madock only scoffed, looking unimpressed by Jeremiah's performance.

"Alright, let's get started," Jeremiah said, hiding a smirk.
This is going to be interesting.

It was a long day; training three boys to be soldiers didn't seem like the ideal job, but it was his assignment. He himself wasn't a soldier, yet after having dealt with the problems in the Grey, he understood the need for it. Still, the day was finally over, and with no real progress other than one *man* hitting his target… Barely.

Now, he sat at a table in the saloon with Chamberlain, sipping on his whiskey while his recruits sat at the bar chatting with one another. Chamberlain had barely said a word as he sipped on his amber ale, studying the men who he had assigned to Jeremiah.

Jeremiah wondered what was buzzing in that head of his, even more so after his first day of training the troops. However, he knew if anything was awry he would be the first to hear about it.

Finally, Chamberlain broke the silence; "Seems like morale isn't too bad."

"No, it isn't. I'll say this, one of 'em needs to learn how to take orders."

"Yes," Chamberlain took a sip of his ale, "I figured he'd be a bit of trouble. They all came in together, though they obviously didn't fall through that way. Honestly I don't know where from, or how they got here, but they did. We just need to get them used to the idea that a soldier in the Grey is very different from what it was before."

Jeremiah nodded as he took his glass of whiskey, emptying it into his mouth. He placed the glass on the table and looked at Chamberlain. "They'll get there."

"Don't be afraid to show some authority." He took another sip of his ale, wiping the foam from his mustache immediately after, "Now, not anything drastic, but you're in charge of those three for the time being. If anything happens that you feel you can't handle, we can get the colonel involved. Again, only if you need him."

Jeremiah had yet to meet the colonel; he honestly didn't even know the fort had anyone for second in command with such a few number of troops. But, as Chamberlain had said, this *was* the Grey, and normal society rules didn't really apply. After all, such few number of troops wouldn't be commanded by a general; a general would be looking over a far larger number of men.

This was only slightly comforting, as he knew that these troops needed to be ready for a fight at a moment's notice, and if they couldn't hit a target it would compromise the defenses of the fort. If the defenses of the fort were compromised, the civilians inside would be dead – or worse – and Jeremiah wasn't able to comprehend how he would be able to deal with that hanging around his neck until his dying breath.

He already had enough hanging there, weighing heavy on his soul.

He was so focused on the consequences of him being unable to train the troops that he didn't even notice a figure take a seat next to him until a fresh glass of whiskey slid across the table to meet his hand.

He looked over to see Alexis pulling her hair out of a ponytail. She was wearing a flowing red top with a pair of tight jeans, legs crossed, kicking one naked foot back and forth as her red heels rested on the ground next to her. She winked at Jeremiah, causing him to hide a small smile behind the brim of his glass of whiskey. The ice cubes tapped the side of the glass and his lips in a merry way. Alexis turned to Chamberlain, holding a tall drink of her own.

"Alexis," Chamberlain said with a nod.

"Commander," She said, "I believe you'd be happy to know that your troops all seem to be in good spirits." She smiled, flicking her eyes over to Jeremiah, then back to Chamberlain, "Unfortunately, the other *spirits* won't last much longer. Looks like a resupply is in order sometime soon." She sipped on her glass through a long straw.

"Yes, I've heard were in need of some resupply. Now, looks like we should be able to get a few troops out to Arlington in the next ten days. Think that will do?"

"Well, I guess. We may run out of whiskey, vodka, and coffee by then, but we should still have plenty of food and water. Just don't want the troops to start a riot or something."

Jeremiah sat quietly as they began to deliberate their options, figuring out how to ration some of the luxury items in order to keep the troops happy. However, he wasn't paying attention to that; instead, he was just studying Alexis. Part of him felt wrong about noticing her silky hair, ruby red lips, deep blue eyes. Still, he felt something inside himself wrestling with memories, churning his stomach in an unexpected yet familiar way.

So, he continued to sit, ignoring the room as he felt his heart beat harder and harder in his chest. *Something about this woman, who she is* he thought to himself as Alexis pulled a bit of her hair from her face to behind her ear. Her ears were pierced in a few different areas, sporting different rings and studs from the lobe to the helix. His silent observations were interrupted suddenly.

"Think you could handle it?" Chamberlain said, looking at Jeremiah.

"Handle what?"

"A supply run in a few days. I think it'd be a good exercise for you, as well as the men you're training. Get them out of the fort, run some supplies, might make them listen to you a little better if they don't have the protection of the fort. Now, might not be all three of them going with you, but I am almost going to guarantee one."

As insane as it may have sounded, Chamberlain made perfect sense. After a bit more training, getting those boys out of the fort might help them understand that Jeremiah is in charge of them. Hopefully, that is how it would work.

"I don't think it sounds half bad." He responded.

Alexis turned to look at him, gracing him with her smile.

The following morning brought the birth of the same story as the day before. Jeremiah took his three trainee soldiers, walked them out of the wall, assembled targets, and made them shoot one by one. It would have seemed even with the lessons the day before, none of them had remembered anything they learned, as none of them came remotely close to the targets.

Jeremiah sighed, putting one hand to his forehead and ran it back over his hair, "Alright, looks like we have to start over," He finally said. The men were standing at attention, looking straight ahead.

Well, all except Madock who was looking at Jeremiah with his dark brown eyes.

"Start *over*?" He said, still looking at Jeremiah "What the fuck? How do you expect us to hit such a tiny little target from so far away? Won't we actually be shooting at men and animals at *least* ten times that size? This makes no fucking sense."

Jeremiah let him finish his brief tirade, thinking that once Madock was finished he may actually listen to what Jeremiah had to say. "Now, that makes sense, don't it? Unfortunately, you forgot something." Jeremiah stepped out, pacing in front of his troops, "Now, those tin cans may be small, but they're sittin' still, they ain't shooting back at you. Think about it for just a second; what's going to be harder to hit? An enemy runnin' and duckin', or a tin can on a dirt mound?

"This is an exercise because I want you to be able to focus on a target. You can hit that small target, from this bit of distance, then I'm pretty sure you can at least wound a man runnin' about. Hit those cans, with at least one damn bullet, and we can move on to movin' and shootin'," He looked at all the men as if to say *understood*?

Not one of them responded; no smartass remarks or rebuttals.

Private Martin stepped forward, taking aim with his rifle. The shots flew, steady and easy, over the can.

Another long day Jeremiah thought to himself as he attempted to figure out how he was going to get them to shoot straight.

He watched as each soldier took their shots at the tin cans before them. Larcow showed some promise as he hit the ground only an inch or so away from his target; but again, that was the closest shot he witnessed for the first round they fired.

He decided he could approach the situation in a different manner. First, he helped the soldiers with their firing stance, except for Larcow who already understood how to stand properly (more-or-less). He wanted them to keep their non-dominant foot in front, the dominant foot in back. The butt of the rifles had to remain firmly at the shoulder, while the non-dominant hand steadied the rifle at the forend. He made sure that they looked down the sights with both eyes open at first, showing them how the rifle would jerk ever so slightly with each heartbeat and breath.

Once they understood these concepts (after about two hours of explanation) he allowed them to put them to action. He stood behind each of them as they fired off their five rounds. Martin hit his target two times before it fell off the mound and rolled out of his sights.

Larcow took aim; missing his first shot, but quickly finding the mark with his second. His third and fourth shots were dead on, but his fifth barely missed, leaving a trail of green into the fog behind.

Finally, the last soldier, Madock, stepped forward. He took his aim and fired with great precision. He was only able to fire one shot, causing the can to fly backward and behind the mound.

Jeremiah finally felt as if he had actual soldiers with him. He lit a cigarette with a half-smile, taking the first drag, exhaling it up to the unseen sky. "Alright," He said, pointing out to the targets, "Reset those can's, and let's do it again," He sat down and watched the men walk out to the targets to reset them; patting each other on the back and joking about their shots.

Jeremiah Wash: The Grey

CHAPTER 14

It took an additional two days of training before Jeremiah was satisfied with his recruits shooting at forty paces. He decided to take the fifth day of training for them to take what they learned and shoot at the tin cans from almost seventy-five paces. There were groans from the troublemaker, but he didn't put up much resistance after. Jeremiah was certain that he understood the training was doing some good to his shot.

Other than the distance, the basic principle remained the same; the soldiers took the same stance, same breathing, same aiming. The only other difference was how they aimed at their targets. If they wanted to hit the bottom of the can, they had to aim more towards the top or center of it. If they were aiming for the center, they had to aim barely higher than the can itself. However, Jeremiah didn't tell his troops that.

No, they had to figure that on their own.

He watched through the cigarette smoke that wafted from between his lips, counting their shots, judging their stances.

Martin had definitely understood the form of the stance and breathing, yet he couldn't figure out the positioning of his sights at the new distance. Sure, he was able to get a bullet to barely shave the bottom of the can, causing it to jump up ever so slightly, but that was it. None of his other shots hit the mark, and soon all five cartridges lay smoking at his feet in the dirt.

The other two soldiers had almost the exact same story; one near hit each, four bullets embedded in the dirt before their targets. The taps of debris on the tin became such a well-known sound. The poor aim caused Madock and Martin to grunt or moan as each bullet missed the mark. Larcow simply accepted his defeat without changing expression or breath.

"Alright, again," Jeremiah said, pressing the dying ember of one cigarette to the fresh tobacco that was frayed out of the end of another.

"Bull." Private Madock said, "We can shoot, and you know it. Why the hell are we just adding distance to a target we can hit? You can barely see it in this shit!"

"Madock," A voice called from the wall above the men. They cocked their heads upward as they turned, Jeremiah included. Their gazes were greeted by a lone figure, standing at parade rest, looking down as if he were the eye of God. "Give me five laps, around the fort." He called out.

Madock grunted, pulling his rifle from his back before leaning it against the wall. Then, he set out, jogging toward the gate, turning the corner and disappearing behind the wall.

Jeremiah looked up, the figure was walking along the wall, watching Madock before he too disappeared from sight for a brief moment. He tried to figure out who the man was, why his voice boomed with such force, and how his eyes seemed to burn through the fog. He wasn't allowed much time to ponder before the figure reappeared from the gate, walking toward the three of them.

"Wash," the man said, "I don't want to impose on your training exercise, but I believe you must learn to keep your troops in order." He removed a pair of fine white gloves before extending a hand out to Jeremiah, "Colonel Radikkt."

Jeremiah took the man's hand in a firm handshake, fingertips extending to his wrist. Radikkt was a goliath among man, standing at almost six-and-a-half feet tall. No matter how Jeremiah stood, Radikkt was looking down. White teeth penetrating through his dark brown lips in a casual, yet imposing smile. He wore no uniform as far as Jeremiah could tell; bare chest barely hidden under an open yellow jacket with silver shined buttons. His pants red, flaring out slightly to the sides just above the knee before forming to the ankles. His skin was dark as tanned leather, burned by the flames of a fire that could never be extinguished.

"Thank you, colonel." He said as their hands parted, "I'm sorry for my man's behavior, he just don't seem to like being told how to shoot."

"That isn't the only thing he doesn't like." Radikkt crossed his arms in front of his boulder-like chest, "Unfortunately, private Madock does not appreciate a civilian giving him orders unless that *civilian* is me." He raised his voice as Madock passed on his first lap, sweat beginning to bead on his forehead.

Their eyes met as he passed by. Radikkt gave Madock a smile before turning and beginning to pace in front of the remaining two soldiers. "So, I believe it is abundantly clear that this fort will not accept insubordination to any superiors assigned to you; civilian or otherwise." His voice boomed, echoing through the air.

"Yes, *sir!*" The two soldiers yelled, snapping to attention. Rigid as two posts supporting the wall.

"Good," Radikkt said. He studied the troops, looking them from boots to eyes, checking their uniforms and demanding their weapons one by one.

Jeremiah watched as Radikkt stood in front of Larcow, inspecting his rifle as if the defects would be microscopic before thrusting it back into his hands. Then he did the same to Martin, and finally picking up Madock's rifle for yet another inspection. He turned to Jeremiah, approaching with his hulking mass. "Your troop's weaponry appears to be in order. Now, if they are to give you any more grievance about your training, feel free to fetch me from my quarters."

Jeremiah snapped to a loose attention, giving Radikkt a salute.

Radikkt returned the favor with his own mechanical salute before turning to disappear back inside the fort.

Madock passed a second time, just as Radikkt had taken his leave. Jeremiah watched him pass by before calling out, "Three to go! We don't have all day, still, gotta shoot some more!"

That first day of shooting at seventy-five paces would end like any other; a stiff drink and a good meal. Yes, it was just another normal day in the fort that stood lonely in the fog of the Grey. Just like his other days there, he enjoyed his evenings in the saloon, laughing with Alexis.

Her voice was a song to his ears, her presence a blessing in the fort. She would share her personal stash of alcohol with him so she could make sure the other soldiers could have their fill. She had also introduced him to a drink she called a *Jack and Coke*. He only ever had one, and he enjoyed the new yet familiar taste on his tongue. However, he told her he didn't like it at all, as she had told him *Coke* was very hard to find, and she could only obtain a few cans.

She could light up any situation with her smile, mesmerizing him; enchanting. That feeling in his stomach would flutter and crawl every time he saw her. It was as if his senses were telling him that something was different about this gorgeous woman who sat next to him the nights he had been in the fort. He could never figure out exactly what it was, but it was always there when they would talk.

"So," She said, sipping on her fizzy *Jack and Coke* through a straw, "How did they do today? Getting any better?" Her lips pressed the straw, taking a long gulp as she awaited an answer.

Jeremiah turned to see his three soldiers, sitting at the bar with drinks in hand, hollering and laughing as if the saloon were back home; back in Texas, 1867. He turned back to Alexis who was in the process of refilling her drink. He watched her, waiting for her to finish the task at hand.

Finally, she lifted her glass, holding it chest height with one hand, index finger and thumb on the other squeezing the straw slightly as it greeted her lips. Her face was gently leaning forward, her eyes big and bright looking up from her brow; he could see a smile hidden within the iris'.

"I suppose." He said finally, lifting his own glass to his lips.

She laughed, releasing the straw from her fingers so it could slide down back into the glass and away from her lips; ruby red. "I see, so they are just okay?" She placed her glass on the table, eyes fixed on Jeremiah. It was like she was reading him; memorizing every detail in his face and eyes, turning the page in his book. Her elbow rested next to her glass, as she placed her chin to rest on her palm. The smile faded to a simper, her eyes just as wide. She didn't say another word, just continued to study Jeremiah.

"Yes?" He said, his glass halfway between his lips and the table on its way back down. Something in her eyes and etched in her lips he knew he was well acquainted with, yet it seemed so foreign; for some reason, he couldn't help but smile.

Her eyes met his and she leaned in closer to him, "How about you? How do you feel about this place?" Her voice was low as if someone unseen was listening in on their private conversation.

Jeremiah let the question reverberate for a moment in his mind as if tossed to the side of a bell. *How do I feel about this place? Is that the question?* He couldn't tell. It felt as if she were asking so much more; so much more than a mundane query you ask a new neighbor or guest. "I couldn't tell ya'," He finally mustered, "truthfully. It feels like a home, but I just don't know if it's *my* home."

Her eyes dimmed to a dull hue, darting from her drink to his, that alluring smirk faded behind her dark hair. She sighed as her chin was released from its soft white bed of her palm. She reached for her glass, grasping it with fingertips by the rim, her eyes looking down to the fizzing brown elixir, her brow presented to him with slightly hunched shoulders. He could tell that something he said wasn't sitting right in her mind.

"I'm sorry," she finally said. He supposed it was just the only thing that she could say, but he couldn't be sure.

"No, I'm sorry. Honestly, just with this damn fog, or Grey, or mist – whatever the hell you want to call it – eats at ya' a little. Does that make some sorta sense? But, so far this *is* the closest thing I've had to a home for a while."

There it was, her smile again, hiding itself in plain sight. Honestly, it wasn't as bright as it once had been, yet it was still just as inviting. His heart swayed a moment before returning to its proper place in his chest.

He darted his eyes to his glass as she looked up at him. He could feel the blood rushing to his cheeks, his heart pulsing in his throat; damming any whiskey that may have been flooding its way down his esophagus. That perplexing – yet familiar – feeling in his stomach restated its existence.

"This is really the only thing that I've known since falling through. I suppose I'm just doing what I did before, and it's safe, but I can't help but wonder what else is out there, hiding beyond this fort." She paused a moment, waiting for Jeremiah's eyes to connect with hers, "But then I see those who come in, and I know I'm one of the lucky ones; if you could call it that." She gave him a reassuring smile, the type of smile that you give to someone when you know everything is falling apart but it is going to be for the better in the end.

He nodded, leaning back in his chair, arms crossing his chest, unlit cigarette perched from his lips patiently awaiting an open flame. His eyes focused on the frayed tobacco as it took the flame, producing a jagged ember of orange. The cigarette found his forefinger and thumb, pulling it away from his mouth as a plume of smoke erupted forth. Her eyes disappeared for a moment, giving him a moment's hesitation before speaking, "Ya' must be one of the lucky ones."

She cast her eyes down to the table, her hand began to tremble as it reached for her glass. Jeremiah could tell there were tears welling in those eyes drenched with blue. He reached out, softly taking her hand in his; it was soft as fine cotton, warm and inviting.

Hesitation arose in his chest; *what am I doing?* Her fingers intertwined with his, pressing deep into the back of his hand as she pulled his hand upward, pressing her elbow against the smooth cold table. "Can I show you something?" She asked, taking a deep breath.

"Show me somethin'?" he queried, eyes fixed on her still figure.

"Yes… I want to show you something… Something important to me." She stood, still grasping Jeremiah's callus hand, leading him to the stairs hidden behind the door near the bar. She was precarious as she walked, stumbling over invisible barriers. Jeremiah stabilized her with one hand under her right elbow, the other still grasped by her right hand.

Jeremiah stood at Alexis' open door, looking into the small room. Alexis was on her large bed, her torso hanging over the other edge, digging for something from underneath the mattress; her bottom up in the air. He looked about the room, trying to avert his focus from her figure. His eyes darted from painting to painting that adorned the rust colored walls, placed with care to their spaces.

Finally, she sat upright, her hair askew across her face. She blew random strands of hair in an attempt to clear her face, yet they all fell back into place. She laughed, falling back onto her pillow, her drunken giggles being interrupted by indiscriminate snorts.

Jeremiah made his way over, sitting on the pillow-top bed, reaching over to pull the hair from her face. Her laughing slowed, as she turned her head to him; eyes half open, bluer than before in the dim room. She smiled, only allowing him to see her dimples for a brief moment before covering her hand with her mouth.

"I want to show you this." She said, holding the book out to Jeremiah, still keeping her mouth covered.

His eyes remained locked with hers as he took the book from her with one hand, the other began to softly caress her cheek, "What?"

"Just open it, please?"

Jeremiah turned to the book he had placed in his lap, slowly pulling his hand away from her face. He opened the faded black cover slowly, revealing color photos of Alexis. He sat a moment, studying the first page, collecting her features once more in his mind.

She rose from her place in the bed, resting one hand on his shoulder before placing her chin atop it. With her other hand, she pointed at one of the photos on the second page, "That was me, two yeers before I fell through, home in California." Her speech slurred slightly more than it had been when they first entered the room. Jeremiah attributed it to a mix of alcohol and weariness. She turned the page for him, pointing to a picture of her standing in front of a green pickup truck much like the one he spent several nights in, "That was my first ca-" She cut herself off, "Vehicle. It's like a wagon that movess on its own... kinda. But, anyways, that wasss in Hollywood, a short dribe, er, drive from my home."

Jeremiah was quiet as she flipped through the photo book, pointing out different photos of her and her friends, family, sights. She explained every photo as best she could, yet seemed to jumble her words, leaving some of the explanations to trail off to random – usually unrelated - stories. Still, he enjoyed listening to her reminisce about times past, long before the Grey consumed her; when the photographs were living breathing moments of life.

She told him about her days as a high school rebel in Connecticut; how no one in school seemed to think she was intelligent because she caused trouble in class. She tried to explain it was because she was bored in her classes, but it ended up turning into a brief story about how she and her friends smoked cigarettes in the gymnasium one night. He wondered if there might have been any pictures from that night, yet she never pointed any out to be attributed with that particular story.

Then, a pain shot through Jeremiah's soul; had the Grey never taken either of them, he would have been long dead before she took her first breath. He would have never known her kindness, her soft hand or cheek, the way she walked or talked. She would have never known him. It was a strange feeling, thinking about a woman other than his beloved late wife in such a manner. Yet, it still hung, *would she be happier?*

The thoughts and feeling quickly escaped his mind as he felt Alexis' soft lips press against his cheek. He could feel her warm breath leaving her nostrils and entangle with his sideburns. He felt light, even if just for the brief moment, as his heart pulsed through every part of him, flushing his skin. Eyes began to warm, almost burning, as her lips remained attached to his cheek. All of this in a split second of time, a split second that lasted his whole life.

She released her kiss, chuckling quietly to herself as she fell back to her pillow. Her eyes were closed, arms above her head, arched back, smiling while biting her lower lip. Her legs squirmed a moment before halting, her eyes opened halfway in a dance between consciousness and exhaustion. Through every flutter of her eyelids, she directed her soft eyes to his. Her eyes were shimmering, tides of emotions ripping from her mind and being projected into his.

He brought his hand softly down to her cheek once more, before leaning in and pressing his lips against her forehead. His eyes closed as he felt her brow against his lips, his nostrils filled with the scent of pear and clementine's, forcing his mind into the spiral of impossible fantasy and compunction. His eyes battled between tears of pain or of joy, doubt or knowledge, acceptance or dissension.

He drew his head away, opening his eyes to be greeted by her resting features; she had fallen asleep.

Rising from the bed, he pulled the sheets from her feet to cover her up to the neck before turning and slinking out of her door. He closed it quietly before making his way down the stairs and out of the saloon.

B.E. Amestoy

CHAPTER 15

Chamberlain sat quietly reading in his quarters, Jeremiah stood in the corner waiting to be acknowledged. The General had called on him in the middle of his troops third day of training at seventy-five paces, leaving colonel Radikkt in command to take care of more tactical approaches to war. Although Jeremiah may have had a great shot, he had not the slightest idea of how a battle would play out; least of all the best formation or orders for troops to follow in the heat of combat.

Chamberlain finally stacked the papers he was reading, tapping them against the table to correct every edge before placing them neatly on the corner of his desk. He began a hacking cough as he waved Jeremiah to sit with one hand, covering his mouth with the other.

Jeremiah sat himself into a sturdy oak chair, positioning himself to face Chamberlain, waiting for him to begin. The room smelled slightly of charred pine thanks to an old wood burning heater sitting in one corner. The windows were permanently open; the glass broke long ago from some unknown attack or act of vandalism.

"So," Chamberlain said through coughs, "I have something new for you." He opened a drawer on the right-hand side, shuffling his hand about, looking for something.

"What?" Jeremiah felt slightly confused, he already had an assignment; to train the three soldiers who were currently learning tactics from Radikkt. What else could the General want from a civilian?

"Well, you see here," He stood from his chair, beginning to unravel a map he had pulled out from his drawer. The map was very obviously made in the time since the fog consumed everything, probably by scouting parties and visitors. "I need you, as well as three men and a driver, to pick up supplies from Athens. From what we've done before, it should be about a day's drive."

Jeremiah studied the map, taking note of landmarks and certain features seemingly forced into place by random hands. There was a red dot in the center, labeled *Fort*, with random bits of illustration and lines that appeared as spider legs. One of the areas led to a small dot labeled *Athens* in a shaky handwriting. Chamberlain brought a finger down on *Athens* before looking up to meet eyes with Jeremiah.

"Now, from what we have already gathered from past expeditions about this location is that it seems relatively old; as if it, and its inhabitants, have been stuck in the mist for longer than most. The good thing is that they have a good amount of supplies for trade." His cough began once more, forcing him to pull his handkerchief from his pocket.

"So, ya' just want me to go and get some supplies?" Jeremiah kept his eyes on the map, tracing his finger along the route from *Fort* to *Athens* as he spoke. Some of the trail he would take seemed improbable; a complete circle at one point, backtracking at another. Still, he had no reason to question that somebody had to have made this map by experience.

"Yes, it is the closest city that has what we need; water, canned goods, some fresh meat. It also has some other non-essentials such as liquor, coffee, tea, tobacco; really, you just need to ask around for just about anything. We'll load you up with some items to trade, and one of the men will handle negotiations."

"Alright, so where do I come in, General?"

"Just want you to be a lookout; make sure nothing sneaks up on you or the men. I'm sure you already know that the Grey isn't exactly forgiving"

Jeremiah studied the map for another brief moment, contemplating the route and possible dangers that may lay ahead. Still, he had no real experience for bartering or being a courier – aside from the one job he completed with the crew he lost – and couldn't really figure out the best way about the situation. "You said 'a day's drive', but I haven't seen a rig or nothing like that round here. You got one lyin' outa sight?"

"Yes, we do. Out back behind the Saloon is where we keep it; in its own building. Now, Driver won't be too happy with me just throwing you on a crew the day before they're supposed to leave, but he'll manage. Just remember; out on the rig, *he* is in charge. However, once you get to Athens, the negotiator will be in charge."

"Understood, but, sir, why not Dallas? Looks to be quite a bit closer, well as a direct route." He traced an almost straight line from *Fort to Dallas*.

"Well, Dallas is a risk when it comes to trade. Unfortunately, it has been unable to regain any sort of structure since the Grey consumed it. While many couriers do go there, we have a small town to take care of, and cannot afford the possibility of supplies being stolen, or worse." Chamberlain looked at Jeremiah, searching for comprehension in his posture.

There was a brief moment of silence as Jeremiah traced the route to *Athens* once more. Finally, the question that was eating away at his mind came out, "Is this Athens the Greek city?"

Chamberlain gave a brief laugh, sinking his head past his shoulders. "Well, no, not exactly. However," he rested himself back into his seat, massaging his thigh, "It is a little, well, unique in terms of the cities around here."

"Unique?"

"Yes, unique. You see, most people who fall into the Grey typically stay put. Now, the buildings and other items around them might not come with them, but for the most part, you're in the same place. This is typical, however, maybe one out of every hundred people fall through and aren't exactly in the same general area they were before."

"Like Alexis."

"Exactly like Alexis." Chamberlain reached for a canteen, taking a sip before offering it to Jeremiah who waved his hand and shook his head. He was waiting more for Chamberlain to continue his explanation, "You see, this particular location fell through; random buildings, streets, vehicles, yet none of the actual residents have fallen through. Now, I'm not saying no one came through, it's just everyone who's appeared there all came from different parts of the globe; no one from that town.

"This is both a great thing, as well as a burden when it comes to trade and diplomatic affairs. It has been a rocky road, but the residence there have been able to secure items that are very hard to come by, and they are fair in dealing with others. The problem comes in when you are trying to communicate. Half of the merchants don't speak any English, and the majority of the other half can only know basic phrases. But, again, you won't be having to deal with any of that." He paused, reaching for his handkerchief as mucus in his lungs began to rumble with his breath. He forced a cough to pry it free, "That is all"

"But, sir,"

"No," His cough escalated, "Head to the saloon... I'll have Driver meet you there."

Driver was a short, pudgy man, hair graying atop his head. He studied Jeremiah as he paced back and forth, "Sending me a fucking southern boy," he said, "Least they could have done is send me one who knows a damn thing." He made his way to the door, gesturing for Jeremiah to follow, "Well, no use in sitting around here pissing about it, come on."

Jeremiah followed Driver to the back of the saloon, there he
noticed a large opening in the side of a structure he hadn't paid much
mind to since he arrived. Driver walked inside, holding up a hand to stop
Jeremiah short of entering. Jeremiah lit a cigarette and waited a moment,
looking around the fort to the men patrolling the walls. He was startled
by a loud rumble coming from within the structure, turning to see four
glowing orbs creeping forward from the darkness within.

A large pickup truck emerged, hauling a long trailer, detached
from the cab. It didn't look like the rig he had been on at all; no obvious
way from the cab to the trailer.

Driver emerged from the cab, freezing the vehicle to rumble as it
let out small puffs of black smoke. "Alright, get in," he said to Jeremiah
as he rounded the vehicle to the other side. Jeremiah made his way to the
truck, opening the door just being where Driver had emerged. "The Hell
do you think you're doing, Wash?" he called out, "Get in the front!"

Jeremiah slung himself into the front of the cab, being presented
by levers and a wheel as driver muttered to himself. "What now,
Driver?" Jeremiah asked.

"Dammit, the name is Leon. I don't understand why they call all
the fucking rig drivers *Driver*, but it's annoying as Hell."

"Alright… Leon, what now?"

"You're going to learn how to drive this damn thing. One rule
we have on this rig; you learn to drive, or you stay on the fort."

Jeremiah looked at the wheel, the switches, the random letters
and numbers, wondering how any of it worked. He looked over
questioningly to Leon, as if waiting for some explanation as to what to
do. Leon wasn't paying any attention to Jeremiah's confusion, instead, he
was adjusting his seat slowly with a mechanical whirl and clicks.
Jeremiah cleared his throat, catching Leon's attention.

Leon sighed, "That's right, you don't know a damn thing about
cars or trucks. Dammit," He opened his door, stepping out and making
his way over to Jeremiah's side of the vehicle. He could hear the
annoyance in his voice, "So, this is going to take a *lot* fucking longer
than I thought it would."

He pointed to the different parts inside the cab, naming them and
explaining their function. He turned a key, cutting power to the engine,
and explained briefly about its function. Though at the end of his lecture,
he pointed to the two pedals and said: "Basically, these two pedals are
the only thing worth a damn."

After the brief introduction to the workings of the vehicle, Leon made his way back over to his seat and told Jeremiah to turn the ignition. Jeremiah caused the rig to roar to life with the turn of the key, it shook and vibrated the cab. With Leon's instruction, he shifted the gear from *Park* into *Drive*. It lurched forward, causing the two occupants to bob forward and back before it moved forward smoothly.

"Alright, so," Leon began, "The pedal to the right is the gas, push it in slightly to go a little faster, just like I told you before. We aren't going to get up to speed, just go enough to turn the wheel a bit, then break, then I'll park the thing."

Jeremiah pushed the right pedal slightly, causing the needle to move from just below the *5* up to the *10*. He turned the wheel to the right, then to the left, causing the rig to snake around the open ground behind the saloon. As the inside wall of the fort drew closer, he pressed his foot to the left pedal.

"Dammit!" Leon shouted as the rig came to an abrupt halt, "You trying to give me whiplash? Just put the damn thing in park. I don't think you're going to need to drive the damn thing, so get out. I'll deal with the Chamberlain about not teaching you to drive, but I just don't have the damn time to deal with you."

Jeremiah exited the cab as Leon crawled from his seat to the driver's side. He slammed the door shut before Jeremiah could say a word, and then gingerly maneuvered the rig from its location, bringing it back around to the building it resided within. He stood, and watched for a moment before he turned to return to the saloon. With any luck, Alexis would be able to have a conversation, and maybe a drink.

CHAPTER 16

Jeremiah sat on the ground, waiting for the rest of the crew to meet up outside the back of the saloon. He sipped a cup of tea that Alexis had brewed for him that morning. He hadn't expected to stay the night with her in her room, but the conversation had stretched to the point where they became weary from the intellectual stimulation. A smile came across his face, although he had partially begun to fight with himself over the feelings that had begun to burst from his heart; it was nice to have someone care.

His mind reflected back to his Jennifer, causing him to sink his head low into his tea. He lit a cigarette, *till death do us part*. He felt he would have been much older before it came to that; before it came to the sobering realization that she was gone. Still, it somehow felt as if he were breaking that vow. His eyes drew to the gray sky, inhaling the charred, burning tobacco, to exhale it through his nostrils. *I am breaking no vow, none at all.*

His thoughts were interrupted by a familiar, yet unwelcoming voice. "Well, look who's been demoted." Madock appeared from around the corner of the saloon, "I knew I'd be dealing wi-"

"Can it!" Leon called out before Jeremiah could even react, "I have to deal with *two* new people in my damn rig, they will be quiet! Understood?"

"Not on your rig yet," Madock said, leaning against the wall, smirking to the pudgy man.

Leon scowled at Madock, before turning and entering the building that held the rig, leaving Jeremiah and Madock alone to wait for him. They didn't have to wait long before the rumble of the rig echoed off the walls and out into the fort.

Jeremiah rose from the place he had been sitting, pulling his satchel strap up and over his shoulder as he flicked his cigarette to the ground. As the rig pulled out, Madock jumped into the open back where the trailer connected, not waiting for it to stop. Jeremiah looked into his satchel, pulling out his last unopened pack of *Camel* cigarettes. He carefully unwrapped the cellophane, crumpling it and putting it in his pocket. He pulled out a cigarette from the pack, reaching for his matches to light it, but was cut short by a hand holding a silver lighter to the end of the cigarette.

He looked up to see Robinson holding out the lighter, offering

Jeremiah a weak smile, "Wash." He said with a nod as he returned his lighter to his breast pocket, "You think you are ready for this?"

Jeremiah took a drag off his cigarette, nodding slightly to Robinson. He knew he wasn't completely ready for whatever may lay ahead, but then again he wasn't ready for the Grey to hit, nor was he ready for anything that has happened since then. Still, he felt confident that Chamberlain had made the right decision in sending him off with the crew to obtain supplies.

He counted the heads around him; three, including him, as well as Leon. One of the crew still wasn't present. It was still early, at least as far as he could tell, and there was still plenty of time before they were going to head out to *Athens*.

"Get your asses over here!" Leon yelled to Robinson and Jeremiah, "Inspect fucking everything on this rig, don't want a damn thing going wrong out there."

Jeremiah made his way over with Robinson. Robinson began to kick the tires, and pulling on the sides of the rig. Jeremiah mimicked his movements, as well as checked what supplies were already in the trailer for trading. He rummaged through ammunition and weapons that were stored in the trailer, making sure that it all was in working order and ready for trade. The last thing he wanted was for the weapons to malfunction and have to deal with someone who had felt they had been made a fool from the trade.

"Alright," Chamberlain's voice called from behind the men as they inspected the rig. They all stopped what they were doing, scrambling to get to attention on the side of the rig. "Is everything in order, Driver?"

Leon stepped forward, saluting, "Filled up, ready to go, sir!"

"And, how about the goods to trade?" Chamberlain turned to Robinson.

"Enough to get what is needed, sir! We also were able to obtain some handmade goods from soldiers and citizens."

"Well, if everything is all in order, let's move out, men." Chamberlain entered the front of the truck, the other men piled into different parts of the truck. Jeremiah stood stunned for a moment, wondering why Chamberlain was coming on the excursion to *Athens*. He shook the question from his head, jumping into the open back of the truck, his rifle resting on his lap as he sat down. Madock rested in the rear with him, head on the floor of the trailer, looking up.

The rig lurched forward to a slow crawl, heading towards the gate. Madock took a deep breath and then sighed. "Ah, smell that exhaust. You know, when I come from, people used to say that this shit would destroy the world," He held his hands in an exaggerated manner, chuckling before letting out a ghostly woo, "Well, look at this shit. Worlds ended, and it had nothing to fucking do with my damn exhaust. Suck on that, liberal pricks."

Jeremiah didn't really acknowledge Madock's short rant, he just puffed on the cigarette, watching the tiny fort go by around him. As they began to exit the gate, he recognized Radikkt standing at parade rest. Jeremiah nodded, tipping his hat to him as they passed by. And, with that, the fort was behind them, slowly fading into the mist as the five men ventured out to *Athens*.

Athens came into view as the rig slowed to a steady pace. Jeremiah stood in the back, looking over the cab to the small city, darting his eyes from side to side. He took in the scene; buildings no higher than two stories lined a long straight street. The street was gray, yellow lines running down the center until they disappeared into the mist that engulfed everything in the distance. The city was bustling with life as merchants and citizens walked in and out of the buildings, carrying bags and dragging small sleds with goods. Jeremiah couldn't tell how many people were walking about, but it seemed full of life and activity.

The rig pulled off to the side of the main street, there it settled into a large flat patch of earth where eight other vehicles parked. Madock jumped from the back of the rig, his feet meeting the ground with a small puff of dust and a dull *thud*. Chamberlain and the others made their way out of the cab, stretching in the cool air. Jeremiah could smell the familiar smell of cinnamon baking with apples, but was quickly hit by the harsh scent of fumes from the rig.

Chamberlain approached Jeremiah, clapping him on the shoulder, "You had the easy job, didn't you?" He offered a weak laugh before his cough overpowered it. Robinson ran over, offering Chamberlain a small white pill. He took the pill, throwing it into his mouth and tilting his head back, he sighed, pulling out his canteen for a drink.

"Easy job, sir?" Jeremiah didn't understand what he meant; after all, he had only sat in the back of the rig; there had to be more than just that. Not only that, but they were outside the safe walls of the fort, and Jeremiah could shoot. He was convinced that him defending the rig also applied to the defending the crew once they reached their destination.

"Yes," Robinson said, "You're finished for the day. You just had to keep an eye out on the road, we got it from here. But don't worry, you'll hopefully have an equally uneventful trip back."

"You can stay here with Driver," Chamberlain offered, "Or you can see the town. It is your choice, but," He leaned in close, whispering into Jeremiah's ear, "I'd recommend seeing the town, Driver isn't much for company when he's working on his rig."

He winked to Jeremiah, turning to join Madock who was already unloading some of the supplies.

Robinson began to follow Chamberlain, until he turned back toward Jeremiah, "Think you could butt me?" Robinson said.

Jeremiah gave him a questioning look, raising an eyebrow at his query.

"A smoke. Think I could have a smoke?" Robinson asked, realizing Jeremiah couldn't quite catch his lingo.

Jeremiah grabbed the pack of cigarettes from his satchel, removing one and offering it to Robinson. Robinson took it gratefully, lighting it as soon as it touched his lips.

"Thanks, cat! Oh, and by the way, I forgot to ask you a list of anything you might want while we're here." He fished around in his pockets as he spoke, until he retrieved a small packet of paper and a pencil, "Just jot what you might need down, we'll grab what we can. Also, you have some gold jingling in there, you could grab something if we can't. Just give me the list when you can, we'll be here for a bit." He turned to leave Jeremiah as he went to help the others unloading the assorted goods.

Jeremiah began to write some of the goods he could use; *Cigarettes (lots of 'em), Whiskey, .22 ammunition for S&W Model 1 Revolver, a Canteen.* He knew there was more he could possibly need, but he couldn't think of anything at that particular moment so he wrote, *anything you might think of as useful.* He folded up the piece of paper and made his way over to Robinson.

Robinson stood next to Chamberlain, overviewing the work of Madock as he pulled the last item needed for trade out of the large trailer. Robinson looked to Jeremiah with a meek smile, extending a hand for him to place the list in. Jeremiah reached out, taking Robinson's hand in a covert-pass-handshake.

"Cigarettes and whiskey seem to be the most important, got

plenty of ammo back at the fort." Jeremiah stated as Robinson began to open the list.

Robinson chuckled, nodding as he refolded the list and put it in his left-breast pocket. "Go on, we won't be here too long." He said, waving Jeremiah to the main road just behind him.

Jeremiah walked past, tipping his hat to Chamberlain and Robinson, yet ignoring Madock who was in the middle of cussing and complaining about the supplies he had just unloaded.

Jeremiah turned to walk into town, only able to take a few steps before Chamberlain called after him, "Wash! Keep your weapons here, they don't like weapons unless they are up for sale or trade."

Jeremiah returned to the rig, leaving his weapons in the back of the cab. He felt uneasy without having his rifle and pistol on his person but kept some level of comfort in knowing that he still had his hunting knife.

The streets were alive with chaotic motion; unknown faces shuffling past to the next shop in line. The air was filled with the scent of cooked lamb; seasoned with rosemary, garlic, and thyme. Jeremiah made his way through the robust crowd, dipping away from persistent vendors with thick accents attempting to sell this or that to whoever had a few coins.

He must have weaved through the crowd for thirty minutes, only to make his way twenty-or-so meters into the street. It was as if fighting a strong headwind from a storm as one made their way across a lonesome prairie. He pushed himself into the door of a small permanent structure, being greeted by the smell of green tea steeping in a lone pot on a counter. The shop keeper's back was turned away from Jeremiah. His cloak, a crimson, concealed any features of his body structure. Off in the corner, a child sat, eyes closed as if in a deep meditative state.

"We're closed," a commanding, yet shaky voice came from the cloaked figure, "Please exit at once."

The figure turned to face Jeremiah, allowing their face and color to come into view. He was an older man, eyes dark gray behind bushy white eyebrows. His skin wrinkled and sagging, his cheekbones accentuated behind the loose skin. He raised a hand, pointing with four shaky fingers to the door.

"No," The child said from the corner, his head still lulled back, eyes closed, "He could use counsel; his future is absolutely fascinating," He took a deep breath through his nose, "I can smell it."

The child straightened himself out, opening his eyes; they were calm, an orange-gold. He looked to Jeremiah, then gestured a hand to the chair across the table from him.

Jeremiah felt uneasy from the tone of the boy's voice, and he wanted to back away and through the old wood door he entered, yet he found his feet moved towards the table as if a hand was pushing him forward. He slid the steel chair across the worn planks of the floor with, it screamed out a high pitched shriek for the few inches it skidded. He sat, facing the child.

"Adam," The boy said, his eyes remaining on Jeremiah, "Would you please bring a kettle and a cup for our visitor."

There was scuffling from behind Jeremiah; porcelain and steel clanging about as wooden cabinets creaked open and closed. Yet, Jeremiah kept his eyes fixed on the child. A brief moment passed of chilling silence, not even the sounds of the vendors from outside penetrated the sturdy walls of the building.

Finally, a tea kettle and a small cup were placed before them at the center of the table by the old man's shaky hands.

"Now, may I have your name?" The boy asked, his hands patting silently on the table.

Jeremiah was silent a moment, contemplating what may be happening. His eyes locked with the child's, "Jeremiah."

"Now, Jeremiah, pour yourself a cup of tea; swirl it, take a sip, and then place it back on the table."

"Why?"

"So I may tell you your future, Jeremiah. I can see many demons fighting inside of you, I believe I can help."

Jeremiah hesitated, his mind rushing, his throat began to turn to the desert in summer. Slowly, he reached for the kettle, never letting up his gaze from the child. He tipped the kettle to pour the tea into the small porcelain cup in front of him. The steam thickened the air as he poured.

Jeremiah did as the child said; taking a small sip before placing the cup back on the table. The child reached for the cup, bringing it up to his eye level. Jeremiah watched as the child's eyes followed the steam as it rose above the rim.

"Ah, yes." He said, his voice soft and calm, "The road is long, treacherous, painful. A gust of wind speaks in green and gray, pale. I see the slaughtered, and the one to be destroyed by your hand. *Mulier.*

Susurratio. Cultro. Ah, yes. You seek vengeance; beautiful, hopeful vengeance. Beware of her child, the way it may feed and mature.

"An explosion of some kind, it will release the hilt from Jupiter for Mars. You will fall so far into darkness, but fear not the voice that leads you away from it. Embrace it. Ah, this is fascinating," He leaned in closer, his nose almost touching the cup, "A boy; dead and alive. He steadies your aim, and pulls the Angel of Death away from you."

The boy's eyes grew wide. He recoiled from the cup, looking at Jeremiah with fear and pain. "What?" Jeremiah asked, glancing from the cup to the boy. He knew something wasn't right.

"Well," his voice quaked, "The City of Knowledge... That is where a man of electricity will forage your tool of destruction alongside Mars and Jupiter... And then you will slay that which has brought you here, in the graveyard of steel and petrol. Finding it all thanks to a black bird."

The child began to twitch, followed by a full convulsion causing him to fall to the floor. Jeremiah stood quickly, but before he could take a step toward the child, the old man was in front of him, ushering him through the door. "Yes, yes, you have overstayed your welcome."

Jeremiah was on the street. He turned to re-enter the building, but the door slammed in his face. He jiggled the handle, trying to force his way in. "What happened?" He started screaming, demanding answers; yet the door remained shut and locked. He felt a hand on his shoulder, causing him to spin on his heel.

"Woah!" Robinson said, "Relax there, are you alright?"

"I don't know, but I need-"

"Stop. Relax. They don't like commotion." Jeremiah looked up, noticing the activity around him had paused; eyes all fixed on him. "Just, go back to the rig, we'll meet you there."

B.E. Amestoy

<u>CHAPTER 17</u>

Jeremiah waited for the team to return as he lay in the open back of the rig. Luckily he was able to get a few hours of sleep where he had settled himself; though it wasn't exactly restful. He had already smoked the rest of his pack as he watched the child squirm and shake on the floor over and over in his mind. Unfortunately, it was his words that made him feel more uneasy, as well as the calm tone in his voice until the mention of Jeremiah's own death. *What the Hell did that kid mean by any of it*, he kept asking himself. Without nicotine to calm his nerves, he began to fiddle with his weapons, cleaning them one by one.

It wasn't long before his thoughts and cleaning were interrupted by the familiar voices of Chamberlain, Robinson, and Madock as they approached the rig. He sat up to see them accompanied by six other men dragging sleds of supplies behind them. Jeremiah began to put his pistol back together as Robinson reached the rig. He opened the large steel ramp on the trailer before making his way over to where Jeremiah sat.

"Wash," He said as he reached him. He had two large bags in his hands, causing his shoulders to slump slightly with the weight. He lifted one of the duffle bags into the truck, "That's everything you asked for, you can also keep that gunnysack." He made his way to the cab, where he left the other bag before returning to the trailer.

Jeremiah untied the sack, looking inside to the random items that Robinson was able to pick up for him. He found two cartons of *Camel* cigarettes, some loose tobacco (maybe about half a pound) with rolling papers, ammunition for his pistol, a rusted silver canteen, whiskey, a small vile labeled *Pain Killers* in sloppy handwriting, and a random assortment of clothing. He took a pinch of tobacco as well as one of the papers to roll himself a cigarette as he watched the strangers load the random assortment of supplies into the large trailer.

Madock was the only one of the men from the fort who helped in the loading process, and even then he was just pointing at the supplies to be loaded next. Barrels were rolled in, followed by large wooden crates, raw materials, food, and so much more.

Chamberlain made his way over to the cab, leaving Robinson to watch over the loading process. Jeremiah caught the eye of Madock for a moment as he lit his cigarette, the smoke blocking out the scowl Madock shot in his direction.

"Well, we're all here," Chamberlain said to Jeremiah,

"Unfortunately that means your long break is over, Wash. Think you're ready for the drive back?"

"Yes, sir," Jeremiah responded, his eyes darting from Chamberlain back to the trailer.

He noticed that Chamberlain's eyes were drained of color, the weight of little sleep and tough negotiations was the likely culprit. Black circles hung low, exaggerating the length and depth of his cheekbones to that of a skeleton. Jeremiah knew that the General needed sleep, and also knew that he would be depending on Jeremiah to be on watch as he did so.

"Good. Robinson told me you had a mishap in the town, just glad to know you're not getting into too much trouble. Would have hated to bail you from this towns jail."

"No sir, all is fine, just didn't know what was going on. Nothin to worry about."

Chamberlain gave Jeremiah a nod before he took his leave to the inside of the cab. As the door was closed Jeremiah rose from the back of the rig, jumping over the small side to meet the dusty ground. He walked over to the trailer, flicking the butt of his hand-rolled cigarette off to the side. He felt like he could do more to help than just sitting around while Madock and the six strangers worked; after all, there were still three and a half sleds full of supplies that needed to be loaded up into the trailer. Before he could lift his first item, he was interrupted by a hand on his shoulder, pulling him abruptly from his half-crouch.

"This is my job, get your ass back to glory-boy guard duty," Madock's eyes shot knives at Jeremiah, causing him to stand dumbfounded for a moment, "You heard me!" Madock's voice raised.

Jeremiah held his hands up as if in surrender as he took two steps back, "Sorry, just figured we cou-"

"I don't care what you figured, *glory-boy*, don't step on my fucking toes!"

Jeremiah knew there was no use in arguing with the obviously upset Madock, no matter how much help he could be. He began to make his way back to where he had rested, avoiding the eyes of the strangers, but glancing up to Robinson as he passed by him. Robinson gave him a slight nod as if knowing what Jeremiah wanted to accomplish. Still, there was no use in arguing with an irate Madock.

Jeremiah slung himself over the side of the rig, back to the large opening where he had once rested. He knew that as soon as they were finished loading up, he would be on duty for the long – and hopefully uneventful – drive back to the fort.

The rig jostled and bumped about as they made their way back to solid tarmac. Jeremiah was alone in the back of the rig, as Madock decided to ride in the cab and sleep along with Chamberlain and Robinson. The only men still awake seemed to be Jeremiah and Leon, and although there may have been heavy eyelids, neither let sleep overtake them; after all, it was their job to stay awake.

Jeremiah felt the wind rushing against his face; with his eyes closed, it was almost as if being on horseback again. He knew he couldn't rest his mind in that thought for long, and his eyes needed to continue scanning the surroundings, but that brief thought of the past relaxed him. With a quick jolt from the trailer, he opened his eyes to continue his duty.

He tried to make sense of the featureless surroundings, trying to find anything amiss that could lead to trouble for the small crew. Nothing seemed to stir in the surrounding area as the rig shook and shimmied across the dirt and gravel road that would lead them to more civilized driving. Its engine whined and growled, casting black smoke out from behind Jeremiah, mixing in with the red dust that it kicked up with its tires before it all disappeared into the surrounding mist.

As the solid road appeared in the distance, Jeremiah felt goosebumps run up his spine; penetrating his mind with a chill. He heard a whisper from behind him, though he was unable to understand the words or even recognize the voice. *Was it a man? Was it a woman? A child, elder, or maybe something unknown?* He checked from the corner of his eye, trying to take a look at any figure that may have made their way onto the rig without turning his head; a figure sat just behind and to the left of Jeremiah.

He took a deep breath, positioning his finger to the trigger of his rifle slowly. He did his bests to keep all of his motions natural as if he hadn't noticed the figure; he wanted to maintain the element of surprise. He counted to three in his head before spinning on his heel to face the unknown hitchhiker who had been able to jump onto the moving rig without alerting Jeremiah. There, down the barrel of his rifle, he saw no one where there had once sat a person.

Jeremiah lowered his weapon, blinking rapidly in surprise. *Perhaps I just need some sleep* he thought to himself as he rubbed his eyes to the bridge of his nose with his thumb and forefinger. Through the dots and blobs that appeared as he re-opened his eyes, the figure sat once more, facing out to the vast nothingness. Before Jeremiah could raise his rifle, it had vanished once more. He stepped slowly toward where the figure was sitting, waving his hand where the head should be just to make sure there was nothing there. His hand moved through the air with no resistance.

Suddenly, another voice seemed to pierce the rushing wind and engine noise. Jeremiah froze; this voice was all too familiar to him, pulling at his heart strings, a lump forming in his throat. He slowly turned his head to face where the voice had come from; a figure stood there just long enough for him to catch its form before mixing in with the surrounding fog.

Jeremiah began to hyperventilate, his vision blurred and wavered; something was terribly wrong. The figure kept appearing, just out of the corner of his eye, yet as soon as he turned to meet it, it vanished once again.

He felt dizzy, falling to his knees. Suddenly the whispering became a chorus of voices, chanting, yelling at him in different languages and accents.

Nws coj peb mus deb lawm
Ze nam ons weg

Gurekin hartu zuen kanpoan

The chanting grew louder and louder. He covered his ears, putting his head in-between his legs. Shadowed feet appeared to surround him. He tried to reach for his rifle, yet he was immobilized by unseen hands that gently touched his back. Finally, he heard the voices in plain English; *She took us, she took us...*

The voices were those of children.

His eyes began to tunnel, his rifle the only thing in view. With all his will, he was able to reach out to it, his fingertips gently touching the barrel. He recoiled from it; the barrel felt as if it were on fire, searing his fingertips, forcing his hand back to his ear to block out the noise. A simple blue smoke began to rise from out of the rigs floor, swirling before him; unaffected by the wind that blasted against the rig.

Suddenly, the voices ceased, their hands no longer against his back, their feet disappearing into nothingness. The blue mist took on a human shape, stepping towards Jeremiah. It extended one hand to touch his head, but before it could, it dissipated back to nothingness.

Jeremiah fell back, leaning against the cab. His breath slowly began to return to normal, his vision allowing him to see everything still in place. With an abrupt bump of the rig, he scrambled over to his rifle, rising to his feet to scan the rig for any signs of damage or intrusion. Nothing. He checked one side of the rig to the next, attempting to make some sense of what had happened. His fingers still felt as if they were on fire, the tips red as the sunset.

Jeremiah was still slightly shaken up as he stepped into the saloon and took his seat in the back corner. He hadn't even had time to take off his hat before Alexis greeted him with a hug from behind. He was still a little jumpy, but he had done his best to hide it from her. He was back in the fort, no reason to be afraid of whatever it was that was out there.

"How was the drive?" She asked, "haven't seen you in two days. I missed you."

Jeremiah felt that perplexing warmth by her words. He wanted to tell her about the town, about the child who gave him an unsavory fortune, about the figures disappearing on the rig as they chanted. Yet, he knew any of that would make her worry.

"Wasn't too bad," he responded, keeping his voice from deceiving him.

She gave him a kiss on the cheek, "I'll bring you a drink," the door creaked open, Madock and another soldier that Jeremiah had only seen in passing entered the bar; stumbling from a few drinks already had outside the bar, "And it looks like I have some more people to be serving."

"Thank you, sweetheart." He said, giving her a slight smile before he exhaled his poison into the air. She smiled at Jeremiah before running to behind the bar just as Madock and the other soldier sat down.

As soon she had left him alone, Chamberlain entered the saloon. A new cigarette found Jeremiah's lips as soon as Chamberlain seated himself to the chair opposite him. He wiped the sleep from his eyes, "Uneventful, as always; at least from my point of view. Didn't have to stop on the way, didn't have to stop on the way back."

"Sir," Jeremiah said with a nod through a puff of smoke, "Uneventful as it could've been, I suppose."

Chamberlain studied Jeremiah's face for a moment, his brow furrowed, "Something happen on the road, Wash?"

Alexis came over, bringing an ale for Chamberlain, a glass of whiskey for Jeremiah. They both nodded to her before she was called away by the soldiers sitting at the bar. She hurried away, leaving them with their drinks. Jeremiah lifted his whiskey up to his lips, but before he could take a sip he noted Chamberlains concerned look. He sighed into his glass, "Nothin' of concern. Just a bit shook up's all." He sipped his whiskey.

"Are you sure? I need a clear head from you." He leaned slightly on the table with one arm, "I can't be having you keeping secrets if it concerns the safety of our fort, as well as all those who are here. You already had the one issue when you arrived, don't want you to be having another."

"Nothin' of concern, trust me. Just had a rough time out there, that's all. Maybe I need to get some more shut eye."

"Maybe."

There were loud hoots and hollers from the two soldiers at the bar. Chamberlain turned in his seat to see that they had been joined by yet another soldier, and were causing a ruckus as they drank and began to slap one another on the shoulders and knees. As Chamberlain turned back to Jeremiah, an eruption of laughter could be heard from the bar as one of them called out to Alexis.

"Damn, didn't peg them for the rowdy type," Jeremiah said as he extinguished his cigarette into the small red porcelain bowl in the center of the table.

"Soldiers," Chamberlain replied, "Always rowdy when you give them leave; even if it isn't *really* leave." He sipped his ale, pausing the glass at his lips before returning it to the table. He could tell Jeremiah's eyes were fixed past his shoulder and to the commotion at the bar. He noted Jeremiah's hand slowly reaching for his pistol. Chamberlain extended a hand to Jeremiah, making him pause before he could reach the gun, "I'll take care of them, you relax." With that Chamberlain got up with his ale, walking over to the troops at the bar.

The men were not just rowdy, but they were also void of any manners. As Alexis handed one a beer, Madock smacked her on the behind; when she turned to scold him, another pinched her. Chamberlain placed his beer down on the bar and confronted the soldiers. Jeremiah couldn't make out much of the exchange at first, but it didn't take long for the confrontation to escalate.

"I said I need you to leave the saloon, soldier!" Chamberlain hollered, "That's an order!"

"Fuck off!" One of the soldiers yelled back, "We're on leave, that means I ain't taking fucking commands!"

"Yea!" Maddock and the other soldier called. They all tipped back their beers, waiting for a refill from Alexis.

"I will have a court-martial for all o- all o-" Chamberlain was cut short by a coughing fit, causing him to lose balance for a moment, only to catch himself on a chair. The soldiers began to laugh at Chamberlain's inability to maintain his footing.

Alexis tried to make her way past the confrontation with a fresh glass of whiskey for Jeremiah, unfortunately, Madock apprehended her. "Hey, you! What? Don't worry about your boyfriend, he won't mind if you stay here with us." He pulled her onto his lap as she squirmed to get free, spilling the whiskey onto the floor.

Jeremiah stood from his seat, walking toward the disrespectful so-called soldiers, fire in his eyes, hand on his pistol. He could see the fear reflecting from her eyes as Madock buried his face into her clavicle. Chamberlain's coughing fit continued, his right hand covering his mouth as he tried to bring himself back to his feet.

"Y'all need to cut this shit out, right now." Jeremiah snapped sternly.

"Fuck off, just having some fun," Madock said as he planted himself down in a seat, pulling Alexis on top of him. She struggled, pushing and slapping him, trying to pull herself away.

"Wanna try to show some respect to the young lady?"

"I. Said. Fuck. Off." Madock said, not even looking to Jeremiah as he began to bury his face into Alexis' shoulder once more. Wash could see tears stream down her face. He pulled his sidearm and placed the barrel on Madock's thigh; making sure it was as far away from Alexis as possible before he pulled the trigger.

Immediately, the man released Alexis, who ran into the back room as he shouted in pain holding his bleeding thigh.

Jeremiah didn't flinch, didn't move; his face stern. He grabbed the man's sidearm before he could react, "Anyone else wanna try to do something stupid?" He said, looking around at the stunned faces of the other troops. No one said a word; they just shuffled out the door and to the barracks, leaving their injured friend behind. Chamberlain regained his composure and walked over, grabbing Madock, and helped him to his feet. He nodded to Jeremiah as he escorted the limping soldier out the door.

Jeremiah made his way to the upstairs of the saloon, finding

Alexis outside of her room; her head buried in her knees as tears poured to the floor. She looked up to see Jeremiah and instantly ran into his arms, allowing his shirt to absorb the streams that ran from her eyes. He did his best to comfort her, rocking her back and forth, side to side. He smoothed her hair, and kissed her softly on the head; he had to make sure she was alright.

Jeremiah Wash: The Grey

CHAPTER 18

Jeremiah stood outside of his home, the Texas air filling his lungs. The sky was clear, red and orange streaked to a deep purple as night began to fall. The dirt solid beneath his feet, birds sang off in some distant nest; there was no evidence of the mist swirling about in any direction. He saw his horse tied up at its post, the chickens locked in their coop.

Cautiously, he made his way up to the front door, hesitation fell prior to each step. He felt his heart racing, his breathing becoming more staggered, knees trembling. His hand reached out to open the door. His eyes were fixed for a moment; the solid wood door was well worn and used. Small splinters formed a slight bristle on the top right corner, nicks and scratches spread incoherently along its surface. He paused, turning his head so his ear faced the closed door. He listened. His blood coursed through the veins in his ears, the slosh with each beat was all he could hear. His palm pressed against the door, causing it to wiggle in its frame. One long exhale, and then he pushed the door open.

His house was exactly as he remembered it, nothing out of place or unknown was in his field of vision. His right heel slowly came to meet the wood floor; there was a squeaky floorboard precisely where it should have been.

"Jeremiah?" A familiar, sweet, loving voice called to him from the other room, "Is that you?"

His blood froze, his hands instantly clenched to fists; Jennifer... He never thought he would hear that sweet voice again, yet it seemed as if everything was the same; maybe the Grey was all just a dream from his fall...

"Honey, could you come in here?" She said from beyond the wall that separated them. It wasn't muffled in the slightest as if she were standing right next to him as she spoke, yet he knew where the voice originated from.

He contemplated a moment, a debate between running out the door and into the Texas sunset or to the room. Finally, he came to a concrete decision; he knew what to do.

He walked through the door, his wife's back faced him as she sat in an old wooden chair. She looked over her shoulder, her blue eyes melting his heart with joy, "Well," She said in a high pitched, serene voice. "Look who is here, it's daddy!"

Jeremiah lit up, making his way over to his wife. In her arms, she cradled a bundle of blankets, a sleeping newborn wrapped within them. He knelt down, one hand resting on his wife's knee, the other reaching to the bundle of blankets. His hand unwrapped part of the blanket, exposing the back of the newborn's head, butterflies infected his stomach. It was his beloved son, just as he knew him after he was born.

"Let's see daddy!" She said, that same inflection in her voice.

She turned the child to face Jeremiah, his eyes were closed; he looked so peaceful. Jeremiah let a smile crack his face, he held out his hands, wanting to take his son into his arms.

His child opened his eyes; the color not blue as they should be, but red as blood. Jeremiah recoiled, bringing his back to press firmly against the wall.

His gaze rose to his wife; blood gurgling in her mouth, yet it did nothing to impede her speech; "What's wrong? It's your baby boy..." She rose to her feet, stepping calmly toward Jeremiah, extending her arms to hold the demon out to him.

With every step, her face began to melt away, leaving more and more of her bare naked muscles showing. The blood dropped to the floor, puddling; extending out to his feet. He scrambled away from her, toward the door to the room. He turned, she was right behind him. Blood. Muscle. Viscera. Bone. The scent of death consumed the room, her skeletal structure began to show. "It's your baby boy... your baby boy... your baby boy..."

Jeremiah scrambled to the front door, swinging it open; his path was blocked by Alexis. She stood, eyes calm. She held up a hand, her index finger and thumb in the shape of a gun pointed at Jeremiah's head.

There was the loud crack of a gunshot.

Blood began to seep from her stomach and through her yellow sundress; she looked down to the fresh bullet hole, then to the pistol in Jeremiah's hand. He dropped the pistol, recoiling; his back bumped into his decaying wife. Both women began to follow him as he ran from window to window, trying to find a way out of the hell that confined him, but to no avail. He collapsed in the corner next to the old wood burning stove. He looked up, hands stretched out to greet him. He closed his eyes, awaiting their touch.

Somewhere, off in the distant prairie, a coyote yelped in pain; calling for something to come rescue it.

The hands stopped just short of Jeremiah. He opened his trembling eyes, the faces of the women were expressionless as they slowly backed away from him. He watched as they parted, turning to face each other, making a space in between them large enough for him to walk through. Before he could stand and run, a figure materialized in blue and green smoke between them; long jade dress flowing in an unfelt breeze.

Whisper crept toward Jeremiah, violet eyes soft yet menacing. She leaned down to him, her cheek pressing against his. "He's my baby boy..." she said before her hand lurched forward to become a vice on Jeremiah's throat...

Jeremiah awoke, gasping for breath, his throat sore. Sweat soaked the simple mattress and sheets, chilling him in the already cold barracks. His chest heaved for breath as he forced himself upright, resting his hands on his forehead. The room felt darker than usual, causing him to feel far more alone than he had been in the time he spent in the fort.

A light breeze swept across the room with a dry heat.

The dream consumed every portion of his mind, filling his head with those painful images. His wife decaying before him, his son a demon, him shooting Alexis before realizing he had drawn his pistol. Tears slowly filled his eyes, rolling down his cheeks to meet the already dampened sheets.

With a deep breath, he cast the sheets aside, exposing his body to the slightly stirring air before he placed his feet to the floor. The steel sucked whatever heat remained in his body away through his feet, causing a shiver to travel up his spine and through all of his extremities.

What the hell... He thought to himself, the images of the dream still encroaching all thought. The hairs on the back of his neck stood on end as Whispers eyes flashed in his mind as her words pierced his ears; *"He's my baby boy..."* He couldn't absorb it all, he couldn't take the pain. He reached for his rifle next to his bed.

The steel of the muzzle was warm against his chin as if it had just been fired mere moments before. His finger found the trigger; quivering in anticipation to release the slug into his brain. He let out a long exhale as a single tear dropped down to the floor.

He was ready.

Before the trigger could be pulled, a blue smoke rushed from nowhere and began to dance and swirl around him. He clenched his eyes shut, doing his best to ignore its warmth as it enveloped him from head to toe. A light penetrated his eyelids.

He felt a small hand press on his shoulder, rubbing in a circular motion as if to console the lamenting soul.

He tried to open his eyes but was stopped by a small voice hushing him. The warmth from the voice penetrated his ears, causing him to slowly pull the barrel of the gun away from his chin. The light faded, the warmth of the hand disappeared from his shoulder; the room became cold once more. He opened his eyes, looking down at the rifle as it rested on his lap; he tried to figure out what had happened.

His mind didn't wander long before it landed on the image of Alexis holding an open wound on her stomach. He shuddered, pulling a cigarette from his satchel. As it met his lips he felt his heart beat slow and his mind ceased to race; a sense of calm came over him for that first inhale. He closed his eyes, laying back on the bed before reopening them to look up at the rust colored ceiling. He knew he had to make a decision, he had to do what was right; no matter what that may be.

Jeremiah had slipped out of the fort during the changing of the guards; his personal belongings packed in two separate bags as well as his satchel. He was slightly over encumbered by the weight of his effects, yet still, he pressed on farther into the Grey. He was well rested, despite the nightmare, and had enough energy to continue on for as long as he may need. He had already been walking away from the fort for several hours, traveling what he assumed to be north, toward Oklahoma.

Out in the mist, Jeremiah could make out a forest materializing ahead of him. He slowed his pace, reminding himself that the forest offers many places to hid for possible hungry beasts of the Grey. He readied his hand on his pistol, kept his eyes and ears vigilant, attempting to find a safe path through the thick forest before him.

As he got closer, he noticed an opening in the trees; black tarmac stretching far beyond sight into the darkness of the woods. He hesitated at the entrance, studying the treetops and trunks, searching for any sign of danger. The scent of wet, decaying leaves filled the air; an almost rosewater undertone attempted to punch through the thick dirt perfume. Nothing seemed out of place, as far has he could tell that is. Yet, Jeremiah had never ventured far into wooded areas if not on horseback, and he was not keen on the idea of entering without some sort of quick mode of transportation.

Unfortunately, he didn't have much of a choice; and he knew it. With a sigh, he dropped his two bags to the soft ground, searching for one of the bottles of whiskey, a canteen of water, extra ammunition, as well as a fresh pack of cigarettes. Once he retrieved the items, he placed them in his satchel and lit a cigarette; better to have them close at hand rather than having to stop to dig for them in the darkened light of the forest. He took one last glance at the opening into the trees, and then back the way he came.

He stepped past the threshold.

The forest was much quieter than the area just outside its green curtain. Jeremiah could hear each of his steps crunch the leaves that had fallen onto the roadway, his own breath echoed off the tall trees. Although quiet, he knew there would be no rest for him for the time he remained in the woods. The tops of the trees disappeared in the thick mist, only allowing the branches a few meters above him to remain visible. The thick trunks had a smooth bark, almost as if something had sanded it down to keep it smooth to the touch.

The ground began to tremble, causing Jeremiah to lose balance and fall off to his side, catching himself with his left arm against the black tarmac. Pain shot up his arm and to his shoulder, causing him to call out in pain. His scream echoed around him, continuing on deep into the forest. He stopped breathing, trying to hear any rustling that could possibly alert him to danger. Fortunately, the only sound he could hear was his own heartbeat.

Jeremiah gathered himself, addressing his arm to make sure it wasn't broken. Although the pain remained, he was confident in the fact that he would only have a bruise in a few days.

He pressed on along the lonely road; walking deeper into the darkening mist.

CHAPTER 19

Jeremiah held a hand to his ear, cupping it in order to capture any distant sound. Somewhere, off in the distance, he heard a muffled cry and shuffling along dried fallen leaves. He eased his rifle from his back and positioned it at his shoulder; left hand at the forend, right hand on the grip, finger at the trigger, barrel down to the ground. He followed the road to get as close to the sound as possible, his feet lightly pressing against the ground.

Heel roll to toe; slowly and cautiously.

The road continued straight into the mist, the sound of crying leading him farther down the path that called him, yet it never seemed to grow any closer.

A wall appeared before him, a rig sitting just inside of a large gate. The wall appeared almost new, built after the Grey struck down the land. Yet, at the same glance, it looked medieval; gray blocks perfectly placed with mortar. He crept around the walls, searching for any signs of life, but was unable to find the slightest hint of human activity other than the wall and the rig.

He looked down the sight of his rifle with both eyes open as he walked fluidly towards the rig. It's faded yellow exterior almost appeared white; the numbers *1022* hand painted on peeling paint that exposed some bare metal. He ran his hand along the rig in front of where the driver would be; it was almost warm.

A child screamed from somewhere within the walls.

His rifle found its way back to his shoulder, his feet carrying him into a large courtyard. There were buildings all around; a city large enough to hold at least a thousand residents. Yet, he heard no sound since the child let out a shrill. He made his way around the city, staying against the wall as he circled. Any open door he came across, he would peer inside. Sometimes he would find nothing, other times he would find tables set with food rotting on its plates as it waited to be consumed.

He continued to circle, slowly making his way inward. He noticed the city was a horseshoe shape; the gate at the opening end of the oblong shape. The structures all appeared as new and well-built as the wall that surrounded them; gray brick and mortar, new and clean glass windows, large wooden doors. He took mental note of every building that had an open door, just in case he needed to find quick shelter.

Fortunately, that wouldn't be necessary as he found himself in a large square; paved to perfection with red and white cobblestones hiding beneath the huddling bodies of what Jeremiah assumed to be the residents of the city. He stood still, silent, assessing the mass that was before him. They all remained knelt, faces touching the cold cobblestone, all in the direction of a very large – and very old – structure.

It was a church, standing tall in the ever thickening mist.

He noted the large stone cross by the entrance of the church. It was roughly the height of the doors, made from a solid piece, without a single imperfection in sight. The other side of the church's door was completely covered by dead vines; they mingled and intertwined along the stones like snakes frozen mid-slither up the wall. From what he could see of the outside structure, it had begun to crack all the way up toward the spire, as if it were splitting the church in half.

He tiptoed through the huddled masses, doing his best to not disturb them from their prayer-like state. Once he reached the steps to the church, he hesitated a moment. The door loomed only six steps above him, it's hinges rusted green, the handle a simple wooden nob. He placed his foot on the first step, the door seemed even more of a colossal blockade. He found himself climbing the steps as if prepared for the Devil himself to be waiting on the other side of the door. He went to reach for the handle, yet stopped dead in his tracks.

Somewhere beyond the door, he heard a child scream out in terror. Jeremiah called out, attempting to see if the child was alright. The only sound that responded was his echoing voice, hoarse and cracked.

The door was heavy as he finally was able to push his body against it. The rusted hinges groaned; unwilling to give an inch from his weight. He heaved his weight again, slamming his shoulder into the wood. He heard it crack, splintering on the other end of the door. He backed up, ready to charge once more, but before he could the sound of the child whimpering came from the other side of the door once more.

He braced for impact, allowing his shoulder to slam against the door once more. This time, it gave no resistance to his weight, its hinges creaking from disuse. The church seemed vacant, the only light being what little pierced the fog through the stain glass windows. There, at the pulpit, he saw a child bent over.

Whispers arms were around the child. Corpses of at least ten young men and women were strewn about the church floor.

"Now, there is no need to cry, my child." Whisper said to the boy, "You are alive, you are well. You've had your fill; now please, it is time to sleep. We will put you back to your place, I promise you.

Mommy is here for you."

The child screamed out, as if in pain before he stood up and faced Whisper. He opened his mouth, only to release a screeching growl that caused Jeremiah to drop to his knees and cover his ears. His rifle rattled against the floor.

Whispers violet eyes turned to face him, a smirk curled up on here pursed lips. "Hello, Jeremiah. Have you come to your senses?"

She stood, taking slow steps towards Jeremiah as he scrambled to retrieve his rifle. Whisper let out a chuckle as the child raced to clinch onto her leg.

Jeremiah steadied his sight onto Whisper as he rose to his feet. "Not another damn step, ya' hear?" His finger rested on the trigger, ready to squeeze and release a lead slug into Whisper.

"Did you not learn, Jeremiah?" She looked down to the child, his eyes fixed on Jeremiah.

Jeremiah glanced down to the child, its iris' red as the blood that dripped down its chin, pupils a sliver of black within. He stepped back, fixing the sight on the child. "It was you! You killed my son!" He yelled out, tears held back by his rocklike resolve.

Whisper stepped in between the rifle and the child. "No, Jeremiah, *you* killed your son. I was simply giving him a new life; a *better* life. You know how dangerous the Grey is, how painful it can be. I was trying to give your son the strength to continue; I adopted him as my own." She looked down at the child behind her, then back to Jeremiah, "In fact; this is the child who would have been your son; *my* son."

Jeremiah squeezed the trigger, striking Whisper in the abdomen; she didn't even flinch as her crystal clear blood spurted forth. Her lips curled in agony for a split second before she erupted in laughter as she looked down at the wound. As her eyes found their way to Jeremiah, he fired once more; the bullet crashing through her skull, liquid erupting from the wound. Whisper fell limp as the child ran toward a window. Jeremiah fired once more, the child fell forward into a pew, blue smoke rose from its wound and rushed into Whispers limp body.

Jeremiah let out a sigh as he lowered his sight.

I've done it he thought to himself as he went to turn on his heel and exit the church. He was stopped mid turn by the cackle of Whisper. He shouldered his rifle once more as he spun to see her rising to her feet, the two bullets that were once in now-healed wounds floated in front of her. Before he could squeeze the trigger of his rifle, it was out of his hands and flying across the room. He reached for his pistol; only to have it follow his rifle and clatter to the floor.

"Now, Jeremiah, that wasn't any way to treat a Goddess," She said, her hands drawing random shapes in the air behind the floating bullets.

He reached for his knife, pulling it from its sheath. As he raised it, one of the bullets flew away from Whisper and penetrated Jeremiah's hand. He dropped the knife next to him, the bullet flattened within its hilt.

Jeremiah cried out in pain, falling to his knees. He looked Whisper in the eye; her teeth gleaming white and jagged from her smile. The second bullet flew from her, ripping into Jeremiah's chest.

Death began to consume him; he did his best to keep his eyes open as he lay limp on the warm wooden floor. "Goodbye, Jeremiah," Whisper said, looming over him. He felt a child's hand over his wound as his eyes closed.

"What do you think?"

"Well, the probability isn't what you would like to hear bu-"

"Just do your work, Aaron! We have a few questions for this one."

"Yes, Driver, I'll make sure I can do everything in my power, but I have to say his heart rate has already dropped drastically, and he has lost so much blood. Even if we can save him, he might not even remember his own name."

"Just do it, I have some questions for him about this Whisper..."

"Daddy..."

The voice was familiar to Jeremiah. Familiar, yet terrifying. He refused to open his eyes, even as a child's hand clasped onto his own.

"Daddy, I know you can hear me. Please, talk to me."

Jeremiah only shook his head, keeping his eyes shut. He lost himself within the pitch of his own eyelids, attempting to escape Bobby's voice. He clenched his jaw so tight that his teeth began to squeal and crackle in pain under the pressure. Still, he refused to open his eyes; after all, this was all a dream.

"Alright, daddy; I'll talk. But please listen.

"Mommy and I miss you, a lot. We know we will see you again, but we also hope it isn't anytime soon. You need to wake up. Please, daddy, wake up. I know it's hard, but I know where you can find her. She ran away to some place with the wreckage of weird buggies.

"Make it right, daddy. I'll be with you."

The hand left Jeremiahs, and the dream became cold and quiet. He wondered if this was the end for a moment before he was jostled awake by the familiar bumping of a moving rig.

CHAPTER 20

Jeremiah opened his eyes, his brain pounding behind them as he felt the unfamiliar rig speeding off into the mist. He went to move his right hand to rub his temples, only to find both his arms and feet being restrained against a barely cushioned cot. He looked straight up to the ceiling, noting its minimal rust and damage.

He was naked from the waist up, a bloody bandage wrapped around his chest, and another around his right hand. His mind wandered back to his encounter with Whisper inside of that church. The rage began to slowly build up inside of him until his thoughts were suddenly interrupted.

"Hello!" A chipper voice said from his left.

He turned his head to find the source of the voice. There, sitting in a small steel chair, was a man that appeared to be more machine than human. His arms were almost an exposed skeletal structure constructed of pure steel, his head with steel along his left cheek.

The man leaned forward, "Glad to see you're finally awake. I am sorry for the unruly restraints, but it is critical to mission success that we understand who you are before allowing you to move freely among the rig."

Jeremiah turned his head in an attempt to study the strange new rig. Unfortunately, it appeared that whoever else was on the rig put curtains around him so he could not see much more than the length of the bed.

"Here you are!" The metal man held out a thin chain with a fired bullet hanging from it. Jeremiah recognized it as a .44 round, possibly fired from his own rifle. "The bullet was mere millimeters away from your heart. I placed it on a necklace for you, as I heard that on Old Earth they used to wear the bullets that had penetrated them in order to protect them from further harm. You almost lost your battle with death, lucky for you we were able to reboot your heart. It is yours, just as soon as Driver has a word with you. Shall I retrieve her?"

"Where are my effects?" Jeremiah asked, his voice coarse as gravel under a rig's tires. His throat felt dry, and he knew he needed to drink.

"Oh, yes," the man replied, pulling a canteen out from a bag that sat under his chair. He walked over to Jeremiah, holding one mechanical hand out to tilt his head up as the other poured the sweet water into his mouth. Jeremiah felt the thirst subside for a moment until the man took the canteen from his lips after only three gulps.

"Your items are all here and accounted for. I attempted to fix your blade, but the bullet seems to have fused into the tang within the hilt. I did, however, use some surgical steel and a rubber-like substance to repair the damage to the hilt, but the bullet remains inside. Stubborn thing.

"Oh! Would you like an apple?" He pulled an apple from his pocket, and before Jeremiah could respond he already had a cut piece inserted into his mouth. "Let me get Driver, she has been waiting anxiously to figure out who you are for almost five days now."

Before Jeremiah could question the man, he vanished behind the curtains. Jeremiah attempted once more to break the bonds that held him to the bed. *Who was he, and why was he more machine than man? Who is this Driver? What does she want with me?* These questions swirled as the mist within his mind.

The rig halted, causing the restraints to groan under the weight of his body as he was shifted in the cot from centrifugal force. He could hear voices, and the shuffling of feet before the curtain at his head was flung open. There stood a woman, her skin a rich chocolate color, her eyes a lighter shade of brown than any he had seen before; they were almost a golden hue like the child in *Athens.* Her curly hair was tied up into a tight ponytail, her clothing simple.

"So, who the bloody hell are you?" She said with a thick Australian accent, her arms crossed across her breast as she walked over to the steel chair that the metallic man once sat.

"What?" Jeremiah responded, caught off-guard by her query.

"You heard me. Now, I need some answers. Let's start with who you are." She scooted the chair closer to the bed, leaning back. Her eyes fixed on Jeremiahs half naked body strapped to the bed.

"Jeremiah."

"Alright, *Jeremiah,* can you explain to me what the fuck happened in that church? All the dead bodies, why no one can remember days, and where exactly *you* came from?" Her voice was stern, pressing.

Jeremiah looked up to see the metallic man as well as two other individuals before he felt the drivers hand turn his head toward her.

"I wish I could tell ya'," he said, his voice losing itself in the rig.

"Well then, I guess I'll just have to make you remember," She began to pull a blade from a sheath on her hip.

"Now, wait a minute!" A voice called from beyond the curtain. "I get it; we don't know who the hell this guy is. But really, Driver, do you think this guy has control over time or something? Look at him, he's normal, just like you and me. Not like he's some new fucking God!" A young man stepped into the small curtained room, his back to Jeremiah. The woman looked up at him, her eyes hard.

"Maybe he is."

"Now, hold on just a second; I ain't no damn god!" Jeremiah called from his restraints. None of the crew acknowledged him as he jostled against the straps, shaking the cot. His wounds began to counter his movements with pain, making him cease his struggles.

"Then why in the hell is he still staying strapped to the bed?" He gestured over to Jeremiah.

"He's right," another voice came. It was a young woman, maybe in here mid-twenties, her clothing functional, almost military. Her hair was short, *very* short. She looked almost to be a young boy who sprouted in the middle of the night. "if he is of the god, then maybe he would be able to take us out. The rig, she is still, eh, moving." Her accent thick with the flair of Southern France.

"*He* is still moving," Driver began, correcting the young French woman about the genders of their non-sentient rig "But that doesn't mean much about this bell end!" She unsheathed her knife, putting it gently against Jeremiah's throat.

"Just fuckin' kill me then," Jeremiah said softly, calmly, no expression of fear on his face, "I'd rather see my boy anyways. I'd rather be able to take her out first. But I suppose if you're gonna kill me, not a damn thing I can do."

"Take *who* out?" The metal man asked, his face etched with concern.

"Whisper."

The knife found its way back into the sheath, Driver nodded at her crew. In one fluid motion, the metal man cut the restraints holding Jeremiah against the bed. He was not expecting any sort of hospitality since he woke up, but he could see a hint of hope in the Drivers eyes. Jeremiah rubbed his wrist, looking around at the crew. "You know of her?" he asked.

"Yes, we know of her," Driver said. She stood up, extending a hand, "Dalia Kessler," Her handshake was rugged, solid, the handshake of a truly strong individual.

The metallic man stepped forward, extending a hand toward Jeremiah, "I'm Aaron!" His voice chipper as when Jeremiah first woke up, "Aaron the cyborg they call me! Nice to meet you, Jeremiah. Would you like another apple?" Before Jeremiah could respond, an apple was thrust into his free – wounded – hand. "Oh! I'm sorry! I forgot!"

"Xavier Erickson," The young man who had initially defended Jeremiah said, giving a nod to Jeremiah.

"I am, errr, Nathalie," The young woman began, "I sorry, am sorry for the restraints."

"Welcome aboard the *1022 BlackBird*," Dalia exclaimed as she exited the small curtained room.

The rig was longer than any he had been in before, yet its width was minuscule compared to the first one he was on. Back when he saved a child's life, back when he lost a child to the Grey. Aaron directed him to the back of the rig to find an area with a place to wash up. The water was very cold, and he couldn't use much of it as instructed by Aaron. Not long after he began to wash his face and arms, the bowl of water turned to a thick brown stew.

It felt good to clean up. The last time he could recall taking any sort of bath or shower was back at the fort, yet he couldn't remember exactly when. He found his shirt and put it on, it's stench looming for a brief second before it quickly subsided.

Jeremiah made his way up to the front of the long open rig. He passed by Nathalie who was engrossed in a novel of some sort as she relaxed smoking a cigarette next to an open window. She paid him no mind as he passed by. He found his way to the front of the rig where Dalia was seated, driving through the mist. He took a seat behind her, crossing his arms on a small wall that separated them.

"Where are we headin'?" He asked, looking out the window.

"To get paid," she said.

Jeremiah leaned back, looking out the window to his left. He pulled a rolled cigarette out of a half empty pack. Before lighting it, he studied the window to attempt to find how it opened. After a moment of studying it, he found two latches at the top, sliding the top half down. He struck a match, shielding it from the wind. He took a drag as he leaned back against the seat. "Get paid for what?"

"Information." She glanced up into the mirror above her head, meeting Jeremiah's eyes just long enough to make him feel uneasy. She turned her attention back to the road as Jeremiah took a drag from his cigarette, "You have info our client wants. We're heading down there now."

Jeremiah's brow furrowed questioningly up at the mirror where he could see her hair bobbing with the rigs movements. "I have it? The hell does that mean?"

"You have info on that Goddess Whisper. We met someone who is-"

"I don't have nothin' useful to give. Just know that I want to put a bullet in 'er head."

"And our client might be able to help. Now, shut up and let me drive, ya' wank."

Jeremiah looked up at the mirror once more, only to catch Dalia glaring daggers in his direction.

He slowly got up from his seat and made his way back to where he had passed by Nathalie. He took a seat across from where she was lounging, waiting for her to find a resting point in her book before he interrupted. Her long muscular legs were exposed from the knee down as they rested on a crate in front of her.

She sighed as she took a final drag of her cigarette before throwing it out the window. Jeremiah took a breath to speak, but before he could say anything Nathalie held up her index finger to pause his thought.

Jeremiah pulled out a cigarette, placing it in his mouth next to the one he was already smoking. He lit it and extended it in the direction of Nathalie. She inhaled deeply before taking a piece of paper to mark her place in the book.

"Thank you," she said as she took the cigarette from Jeremiah.

"Nice rig ya' got," Jeremiah wanted to figure out where they were heading, and he figured Nathalie might be slightly more inviting than Dalia was. However, he questioned that decision after seeing her posture as she smoked and studied him.

"It is," She exhaled the smoke towards Jeremiah, "What is it want, you want?"

"Just curious about the job, the information I have to deliver."

"Yes. Well, you see, it's just a bit of things."

"What things?"

"Her husband, this Whisper, he searches profusely for her."

Jeremiah sat back in his seat, his head lulling back. He perched the cigarette in his lips, mouthing the words *Whispers husband* silently to himself for a moment. His mind raced, trying to figure out how a rogue Goddess has a husband. Suddenly it hit him like the bullet into his chest; *She has a* child, *it makes sense that she has a husband.*

"I see you, you're thinking." Nathalie snapped Jeremiah from his thought process, "He is not target. He not as she is."

"Ya' know how she is, then?"

She picked up her book from her knee, opening to the place she left off as she exhaled a puff of smoke, "We have heard stories; interesting stories. Now, please, leave me to this story. *Au revoir.*"

Jeremiah tipped his hat at Nathalie before standing and leaving her to read her book. If Whisper indeed had a husband who was looking for her, it would make sense that they thought Jeremiah had some of the information they needed. Yet, he felt he would be useless in that endeavor.

CHAPTER 21

Jeremiah didn't get to do much for what felt like three days aboard the *1022 BlackBird*. Dalia kept him confined to the interior of the rig, not allowing him up on overwatch with his rifle for what she said were "safety reasons". It wasn't, however, all that terribly dull aboard the new rig, and all of the crew – with the exception of Dalia – were very welcoming and made enjoyable conversation.

He found Aaron to be the most interesting of the crew, as well as the most enjoyable to be around. Jeremiah learned a lot about how much the world had changed between his time and the time that Aaron fell through and into the Grey. Some would say that he was not quite all there – both figuratively and literally – and he probably would have been lynched in his time for being a demon.

He learned of what Aaron called *The Great Depression*, where many Americans lost jobs and homes; lost their entire livelihood. He learned of the great worldwide wars, nuclear holocaust, political rise and falls, first man on the moon, first man on Mars. Sometimes, though, Aaron would go off on tangents; talking about how the air pollution was no longer at elevated levels, habitability optimal. It was all rather strange to Jeremiah, yet rather intriguing.

Nathalie was a different story altogether. He could tell that she was a tough woman, able to take care of herself; even in the Grey. She didn't have much to say to Jeremiah, yet when she did it was always in broken English, and always concerning the job or client. He couldn't get much out of her when it came to her life before the mist swallowed her, but he could tell she loved her "old" novels.

Xavier was, for the most part, silent unless he felt something absolutely needed to be said. He kept a mask around his neck that reminded Jeremiah of the men who took Sasha and Marie's fathers life. He said that you never know when you needed to breathe fresh, clean air, and you never want to experience what it is like without it. He offered one to Jeremiah at one point, but Jeremiah felt it unnecessary (and was also uneasy by its appearance).

And that was the crew of the *1022 BlackBird* all with their own stories, yet Jeremiah only was able to scratch the surface. A bunch of misfits, heathens, people from different times forced together; not that unusual in the Grey.

He tried to show his worth every time the rig would stop to

refuel or rest. Even though Dalia hated it, he would keep watch, help move canisters; anything that needed to be done. He felt that it was his only chance to maintain his quest to make Whisper pay for what she did to his family.

Finally, on the fourth day aboard the rig, Dalia relinquished control of the wheel to Aaron in order to have a private conversation with Jeremiah. She found him at the back of the rig, reclining on a vinyl seat, cleaning his rifle in silence. When she took a seat next to him, he halted his cleaning and lit a cigarette, "Ma'am," he said, finally acknowledging her with the tip of his hat.

"We'll be arriving at the city in the next couple hours." She rubbed her temples, forcing her eyes shut to eliminate the red that had been seeping into the whites of her eyes, but to no avail. "I radioed ahead, got us a meeting with *him*. All you have to do is tell him what you know."

"What I know? About Whisper?"

"Yes," she leaned forward, rubbing her hands together as if to warm herself, "that's it."

"I don't think I'll be of much use; don't know much 'bout her."

"You know more than we do, and that's something. Look," she leaned back, her hair flattening against the window, "all he wants to know is where his wife is, what she's doing, if he can get her back, or if he needs to stop her."

Jeremiah furrowed his brow, "Stop her?"

"Yes, that is what he said. What that means, I don't know; all I know is you have the information, that's it."

With that, she left him alone once again; alone to ponder at what he would have to say to another God that he believed to not exist. He smoked the cigarette down until it burned the tips of his fingers before returning to the cleaning of his rifle.

The city came out of the mist, pyramids reaching to the sky; gold and turquoise adorning the massive structures. The wall surrounding the city was made of white stones, perfectly placed together without mortar, stretching roughly four-and-a-half meters high. Jeremiah couldn't make out an entrance through the massive walls, yet the rig stopped just outside of the wall.

One by one, the crew of the *1022 Blackbird* departed the rig, laying their weapons on the ground next to the rigs door. Aaron exited first and removed his right hand before holding up his arms above his head. Nathalie was second, leaving three knives, a pistol, a rifle, and a set of spiked brass knuckles. Xavier laid down his two rifles, pistol, and black backpack.

Before Jeremiah could exit, Dalia stopped him. "Lay down your rifle, understand?"

"I figured." He departed the rig, pulling his pistol from his hip, unslinging his rifle, putting his knife to his side and dropping it to the dirt. The air had a slight scent of blueberries and fresh rain, although the ground was dry and dusty beneath his feet. He lifted his arms above his head just as Dalia stepped to the dusty ground. She whistled up at the wall as she discarded her weapons.

Five men, dressed in blue togas, arms covered in black tattoos, presented themselves from the top of the wall. Two held what appeared to be metallic spears, while the other three held rifles, shouldered at the ready.

One called down in Spanish to the small crew, "¿Cuál es su negocio aquí?"

Nathalie yelled out, "Tenemos informatión."

"¿De que?" The other called down.

"Su esposa," she responded.

They could hear murmuring among the men upon the wall. Jeremiah wondered if whatever Nathalie had told them would allow them sanctity inside the walls.

"Abre el portón!" The first of them called out before all five men disappeared from sight.

The bricks of the wall before them began to vibrate before moving on their own accord. They shifted themselves, pulling away from reality and into the other parts of the wall with grunts and groans. Jeremiah watched in awe before Nathalie shook him back to reality with a light punch to the arm. One by one they collected their weapons and boarded their moving home.

Jeremiah took a seat behind Dalia, looking out the front window of the rig. As the rig moved through the opening in the wall, it was greeted by a lush wilderness that covered all of the buildings in the city, including the base of the three massive pyramids. The buildings entrances were all well-kept and free from debris. A small river flowed through the middle of the city, before branching off and connecting to each pyramid at the corner closest to the river.

The pyramids steps were almost glistening from the dew of a fresh spring morning, what little light caught them made them almost twinkle as stars against the dark gray stone. People were walking around freely, dressed in similar attire to the five men who stood atop the wall. Jeremiah could see children playing by the rivers, a man steering a small flock of sheep to the side of the rig as it stopped before the furthest pyramid from the entrance.

The stairs leading up to the top of the pyramid before them had four armed guards at its base, standing in a relaxed yet rigid manner. Their eyes remained fixed on a point past the rig as if looking through it and the lush vegetation to the wall. Dalia sat at the driver's seat, hands on the wheel leaving her knuckles white. She exhaled and inhaled with precision, calming herself. Jeremiah wanted to say something to her, ask her what was causing her such distress; yet he decided against it, holding his tongue behind his teeth.

He opened the window and lit a cigarette. After only two drags, he went to ash it out the window, only to have it extinguished by a single raindrop. He placed his hand out the window, waiting for a few moments, only to have no other raindrops fall from the mist.

"Let's get ready," Dalia said, "he won't want to be kept waiting, especially not with our information."

"Well, fuck it," Xavier said, startling Jeremiah just enough for it to be noticed, "shall we?"

Dalia nodded, releasing her hands from the steering wheel. Jeremiah began to rise to his feet, seeing the crew filing in behind them. None of them had any weapons on them, leaving him to feel he was to do the same. He reluctantly left his rifle in the seat, his pistol in his holster kept it company as they began to exit the rig once more. However, his knife accompanied him out into the vegetated city, hidden in its sheath on his right hip.

They approached the steps one by one, passing the guards as they ascended to the mist above them. Jeremiah felt the air around him enter his lungs with thick humidity and heat. It caught him short of breath, unlike the air outside of the city, this air had a different scent, different taste. It didn't take long for him to take a pause in his steps, lighting a cigarette as he looked up to the gold roof comb above him.

The crew stood outside of the turquoise adorned lintel, intricate carvings depicting storms and rivers being spewed forth by jagged monsters. Jeremiah could not make out anything he could understand, but the others obviously knew something he did not. They stood still, gazing into the open archway, into the pitch darkness it held. They seemed to hardly breathe as they awaited something to happen. Jeremiah wanted to press for an answer to what they were waiting for, but instead just stood silently with them.

As if by some form of unknown magic, the inside of the building lit up with blue and gold light. A throne sat on the farthest wall from the entrance, adorned in the same turquoise and gold as the outside of the massive pyramid.

Dalia nudged Jeremiah, forcing him to stumble slightly forward. He turned, only to catch her tough eyes as she nodded him to enter the grand room. He sighed, turning to the room, and then back to his new comrades. All of them had the same concerned and intrigued look on their faces.

Dalia nodded to him once more, attempting to coerce him into entering. He lifted his right foot, hesitating a moment before he finally went through the threshold.

The rooms bright gold and blue lights blinded him temporarily as the murkiness of the fog had suddenly dispersed. There was nothing other than the throne in the room, no one else dared enter, and there was not another soul to be seen within the walls. Jeremiah inched forward, wanting to pull out his knife but restrained himself from doing so.

"Who has called for audience with me?" A booming voice called to him, rattling his bones and any loose material that lay scattered on the floor. Jeremiah tried to search for a source of the voice, only to be greeted by the same empty walls.

"Name's Jeremiah," He said calmly, still searching for the source of the voice.

"What brings you to my chambers, outsider?"

"I was told I have some information ya' want. Somethin' bout your wife."

The rooms lights flickered before thrusting Jeremiah into complete darkness. He spun around, facing the way he had come; he could not see the outside. It was as if the building had constricted all light from entering. Suddenly, the gold and blue light returned.

"Do you speak the truth?" The voice boomed from where the throne sat behind him.

Jeremiah turned on his heel to finally face his host. There, sitting upon a throne was a young, well-built man. His upper body covered in blue tattoos, depicting the same strange creatures and storms as Jeremiah noticed on the outside of the structure. His skin was darkly tan from what seemed to be many years of working in the sun. From his waist down, he was covered in a very familiar shade of Jade cloth, framed with gold stitching. His hair was long, black as pitch, tied up in a ponytail.

"I guess," Jeremiah responded, taking a step towards the imposing figure.

"You, why do you not bow in my presence?"

Jeremiah stalled his approach, contemplating his next actions or words, "No, I'm afraid not."

The man's eyes narrowed, shooting arrows in Jeremiah's direction before he erupted in tremendous laughter. He slapped his knee, curling his upper body forward. Jeremiah watched, waiting for his laughter to subside. "I suppose I am not your God, and why should I be?" He stood from his seat, "I am Tlaloc, the one who brings rain and storms, causes the ground to allow crops to take root." He slapped his fist to his defined chest, over his heart.

"Pleasure, I'm sure. Now, I don't think my information is of much use."

"I think it shall suffice. But, it is not your information that is going to lead me to her, but your son's."

Jeremiah's blood ran cold, sweat began to bead on his furrowed brow. "The hell do ya' mean by that?" The tone in his voice could have crumbled the structure they stood in.

"Mortal eyes can be so deceitful," Tlaloc waved his hand, causing the light to change to a shade of purple. Jeremiah could feel a small hand take his own.

CHAPTER 22

In the cool purple light, Jeremiahs son, Bobby, stood next to him, grasping his hand tightly. His small figure was transparent, his clothing clinging to his frame. His blue eyes reflected his father's face in them, his smile big and bright. The figure began to blur as Jeremiah's eyes turned to water. He didn't know what to do with the presence of his child. Jeremiah wanted to draw his knife, threaten the God, destroy the witchcraft that caused him to waiver. Still, he felt his heart skip as he looked down to the small hand that held his own.

"Young one," Tlaloc said, breaking Jeremiah's moment of thought, "Please, tell me what it is I should know of my wife."

Bobby opened his mouth, and began to speak, yet Jeremiah could not hear his voice. Bobby continued, and although Jeremiah tried his hardest to understand his facial expressions and body language in order to understand what he was saying, he could not. Yet, Tlaloc seemed to understand every word; nodding and adding in the occasional "Mmm-hmm".

"Why the hell can't I hear my boy?" Jeremiah shouted, interrupting the unheard conversation. Tlaloc, who was resting his chin in one hand, glared at Jeremiah.

"Unfortunately," he finally said with a sigh, "I cannot change the way your mortal ears hear. However, your son tells me of your intentions for when you meet my beloved Chalchiuhtlicue – Whisper is the name she presented to you– and I am wondering how it could be possible."

Bobby tugged on Jeremiahs hand, looking up to him, "What do you mean," Jeremiah asked, as he looked into his son's eyes.

"You wish to kill my wife, yes?" Tlaloc asked, leaning forward.

"Ya' damn right!" Jeremiah's blood began to boil, his fists clenched, "She took my life from me; my boy, my wife. Hell, I woulda' killed her if it weren't for the fuckin' bullet. I will kill her, just as soon as I can figure out how."

"Figure out how?" Tlaloc began to rise, his imposing stature towering over Jeremiah, "You have already been shown the way, and you already have the tool necessary." He gestured to Jeremiah's hip, "The blade" He outstretched a hand, "Please, allow me to see it."

Jeremiah began to reach for the hilt of his knife, stopping himself just short. He took a step toward Tlaloc, "Why? You gonna destroy it?

I'm sorry, but if this is the one thing to kill her, I won't relinquish it to ya'."

"Destroy the tool?" Tlaloc took a step toward Jeremiah, his posture tall and menacing, "Why would I destroy your only weapon that could protect you? I don't think you understand; I'm allowing you to kill her if necessary," He placed a hand on Jeremiah's shoulder, looking him closely in the eye, "Would you like to know what happened; why she now calls herself *Whisper*?"

Dalia paced back and forth outside of the entrance. As soon as Jeremiah broke the threshold, the room went dark from the outside. She wondered what had happened of the newcomer once inside. The only time she had her meeting with Tlaloc, it had been in the town square, in public view after the *1022 Blackbird* had delivered medical supplies after an unfortunate plague diminished the population by 60%. That felt like ages ago, much like the meeting beyond the opening.

"Relax, Driver," Xavier said as he reclined on one of the top steps of the pyramid, "not like standing here pacing back and forth will do much good."

Dalia shot him a glare but was interrupted by Aaron placing his metallic hand on her shoulder. Aaron almost always seemed to have that same smile on his face, it was slightly reassuring. "We can only wait," He said, taking his hand from her shoulder and placing it into his pocket.

"I know, but we don't know if he will give us what we need for a job. You know, if we can get his wife, we won't have to make runs anymore; we could retire *here*. Hell, as much as I love the road, 30 seems to be the oldest I see any other couriers."

"Yup, this line of work sucks balls, I'll agree with that. But really," Xavier stood from the step, "Do you really think anyone retires? What do you think would happen to this city – let alone any other – if it weren't for couriers like us? They'd be fucked; no joke."

Dalia knew that what he said was true, but driving around in the Grey for so long made her feel less human than Aaron was. It's true, the first few months in this Hell were the hardest, but after that, it felt like it was normal. She could kill someone with no problem, steal as necessary, fight anyone without a second guess. And not only that, but she was only about one year away from that thirty-year-old mark.

She looked at her crew, trying to remember how any of them had picked up on this insane life, yet she could only draw blanks. She thought back to the long never ending stretches of road back in Australia.

No, she had to stay in the now. Although this city was well maintained and guarded, you can never let your own guard down while on a job.

"What do you think?" Nathalie said from her seat against the wall, "Think he has something? Like, do he really have what Tlaloc needed?"

Xavier chuckled, "Like hell he does. I bet Tlaloc is getting pissed off right now at the *lack* of information."

"Aww, guys," Aaron chimed in, "I'm sure that Jeremiah is just fine. He probably had useful information he didn't even know he had saved in his memory."

The rest of the crew looked at Aaron in a questioning manner, before Xavier began to laugh heartily. Not long after, Dalia and Nathalie joined in, leaving Aaron to stand alone, trying to understand what he said that would have been considered funny.

It wasn't long before their laughter was interrupted by Jeremiah exiting the throne room, followed closely by Tlaloc. In Jeremiah's hand was his knife, covered in a crystal clear liquid. Dalia's eyes grew large, as she noted Tlaloc had a gash in his chest, oozing with the same liquid.

Before she could say anything, Tlaloc raised a hand, "Now, you must travel. Please, find your way to her, and then return to me. Jeremiah Washington knows what must be done."

Before any of them could ask a question, Tlaloc dissolved into a blue mist that swirled up and out of sight. Jeremiah slowly made his way down the pyramid before the others could react to Tlaloc's disappearance.

"Hey!" Dalia called out, "What the hell? Where are we going?"

"A track, apparently," Jeremiah said, over his shoulder.

Dalia quickened her pace, getting in front of Jeremiah to stop him, "What is the deal with the knife, did you stab him? Is he going to kill you? *Us*? What the fuck is going on?"

Jeremiah's eyes were stern, yet she could see the bloodshot in the whites. Tears had obviously passed down his cheeks. She took a step out of his way, his eyes following her before he continued to descend the pyramid, pulling out a cigarette and lighting it. The smoke from his first puff seemed to hang behind him, waiting to be broken through by the rest of the crew as they followed.

"You think we're going to survive?" Nathalie asked Dalia in a whisper once she had caught up to her. They both kept their eyes fixed on Jeremiah as he descended ahead of them.

"No," Dalia responded in step with Nathalie, "But I can't say the same about him."

"You want to do *what*?" Xavier called from his seat aboard the *1022 BlackBird* as it remained just outside of the pyramid. The crew ate canned cold soup, listening to Jeremiah explain the circumstances of the so-called next job. "Honestly, you've got to be fuckin' shiting me!"

"It doesn't sound that bad," Aaron chimed in.

"Doesn't sound that bad? You have to have some short circuit or something." Xavier began to walk about the small room in the rig, "Honestly, Driver, you can't think this is a good fucking idea. Really, look at us. Fuck, you ever hear of someone – a *mortal* – taking out any God? Because I sure as hell haven't!"

Dalia and Nathalie sat quietly, eating their soup. Xavier waited for Dalia to acknowledge his point of view about the situation, yet she never once looked up. Nathalie whispered something to Dalia as she shot a short glance toward Xavier. "Valid," Dalia said finally, placing her can of soup off to the side.

"The fuck does that mean?" Xavier snapped, his blood boiling.

"Relax, have a seat," Aaron said, placing a hand on Xavier's shoulder only to have it cast away instantly.

"I'm not saying it's a smart idea," Dalia said, looking over at Jeremiah, "But we don't really have much of a damn choice. Now, are you sure that is what Tlaloc said?" Jeremiah nodded as he finished scooping the last of his soup into his mouth, "Well then, maybe we should discuss strategy."

"You. Are. Fucking. Retarded." Xavier shouted, pulling his hair in all directions. "We don't even fucking know this guy hardly. Yes, he has been good to talk to, yes he has helped us with Tlaloc, but for fuck sake." Xavier turned to Jeremiah, "Now, don't get me wrong; I like you, man. You don't bug much, and you got your shit together. But this is just mass amounts of stupid."

Before Jeremiah could respond, Dalia drew Xavier's attention; "I know; you think I like anything about this?" Dalia was now at eye level with Xavier, "But let's face the facts; we have been running around, wearing ourselves thin. We do this job, we can retire, we can *stay* here instead of hitting every town from here to Sydney."

Xavier began to back down, finding himself back to his seat next to the window. Still, he never broke eye contact with Dalia.

"What if we distract her," Nathalie chimed in, causing all eyes to meet hers, "She knows of him, not us. And we have the muscle if you think about it."

"Well," Jeremiah replied, "Either way, let's just get it done. Tlaloc told me how to do this, you don't have to help; y'all can just leave me there to deal with her. After all, this ain't y'alls battle."

"See, we don't have to die – I mean help," Xavier responded.

"Aaron," Dalia said, "Get behind the wheel. I think we should be on our way, but we all need some rest."

"Of course!" Aaron had a massive smile on his face as he made his way to the driver's seat of the rig.

CHAPTER 23

Jeremiah sat on overwatch as the rig sped through old desert roads, and although Xavier was on overwatch with him; the lack of conversation made it feel like he was alone. Jeremiah had no idea where they were going, but it wasn't his duty to drive there. He reclined while keeping a watchful eye on the passing terrain.

Xavier spoke into his shoulder, "Yea... alright... got it... you sure we want to... no, I understand... yeah, I'll let him know..." He turned over to Jeremiah, "Driver wants ya down below. Guess she wants to have a chat. Send Nathalie up when you get down there."

Without another word, Jeremiah made his way to the small hatch that led inside of the rig. He took one last look at Xavier scanning the road ahead before the hatch latched shut.

The inside of the rig was humming with the sound of its engine, almost a comforting song to Jeremiah's ears. He first made his way to find Nathalie, only a few steps from the ladder. As per usual, she was reading an old novel while smoking a long filtered cigarette. He tapped her on the shoulder, only to be greeted by her index finger pointed toward the sky. He stood for a brief second, waiting for her to finish her chapter before he could inform her of Xavier's need for a comrade.

When she finally set the book down on her lap, Dalia had approached Jeremiah from behind, "Nathalie, head up top; keep watch with Xavier for a minute. I need to have a word with Jeremiah here." Nathalie posed no objection to the request and immediately made her way up to over watch.

Jeremiah turned to face Dalia once Nathalie had closed the hatch to overwatch only to see Dalia making her way to the back of the rig. He followed her until they had reached the rear most seats in the rig. Dalia opened a window and lit herself one of Nathalie's cigarettes. Although Jeremiah hadn't known the crew for longer than a few days, this was the first time he had seen Dalia smoke a cigarette.

Jeremiah took his seat across from her, opening a window and lit a cigarette. His eyes fixed on Dalia, waiting for her to begin with whatever it was she wanted to discuss. He noted her gathering her thoughts through closed eyes and exhaled cigarette smoke. He could tell there was a slight quake in her breath, a tremble in her hand as she brought the cigarette to her chapped lips. He took note of the scars on her knuckles, the bruises, and scabs. Dalia was definitely a hard working woman, someone with a life of hardships.

"Do you know why Xavier got so upset?" She finally said, but did not wait for Jeremiah to respond to her query, "Do you know why I was so livid with you when we first met?"

"Can't say I do, aside from the town bein' trashed and then findin' me there," He could feel the heat of that moment burning his mind, charring yet another painful memory forever into it.

"Not exactly," She took a drag off the cigarette, it's amber lighting her face with a devilishly orange glow, "We almost had a home, back in *New Alexandria*; you know, that town we found you in. Honestly, it would have been nice to just get away from all this. But, then whatever happened in that town happened, and we found you. Not only did we find *you*, but we found you surrounded by all the dead."

"But it wasn-"

"The town wanted to hang you, bleed you dry, until we intervened. They weren't exactly thrilled with the idea of the only suspect leaving with us, but we convinced them. *That* is when they told us we couldn't return.

"Before *you,* they offered us a place to retire. All we had to do is run the water to them, and we could have stayed. Xavier just didn't want to get his hands dirty at first, he has plenty of blood on them, but he has no intention of dying." She paused, looking Jeremiah in the eye. The silence seemed to last a lifetime, her gaze as a razor.

"I have no intention of gettin' any of you killed," He finally said, breaking the dark silence. Honestly, Jeremiah had not expected to have companions along when he was finally able to face the one responsible for his family's death. "This is my problem, and I'm sorry for dragin' ya' into it, I really am. But ya' also drug me along. Now, I've been thinkin'; you and your crew can just drop me there, I'll take care of it."

"Afraid I can't do that."

"Why not?"

"Because we need to make sure you succeed. All I ask of you, if you succeed that is, is for you to put in a good word for us with Tlaloc so we can finally have a place to rest our heads. Only way you can do that is if I make sure you're still alive. Understand?"

"I hear ya', but I don't think I am alright with it. Again, I don't need more blood on my hands."

Dalia was silent a moment, taking her final drag from her

cigarette. With the smoke in her lungs, she held her breath a moment, then spoke as she let the cigarette fly out the window, "Looks like you don't have much of a choice," She stood, "And we will make it out of this. After, we can drop you off wherever you'd like."

With that, she walked back to the front of the rig, leaving Jeremiah to his cigarettes. He noticed a flask sitting on the seat where she once sat. He picked it up, shaking it to check how much might be left inside. It was empty.

Aaron had gone past Jeremiah in the back of the rig to the small washroom located at the rear. Jeremiah hardly noticed him passing, as he was lost in his own thoughts. It didn't help much that he had retrieved his bag in order to drink what was left of his whiskey. It had, however, helped relax his mind just enough for him to not stress as much as he felt he should have been.

Jeremiah had sat in the same seat for several hours, waiting for Xavier or Nathalie to return from overwatch, yet that time seemed to never come. Still, with the alcohol now infecting his mind, he figured it was for the best.

"Jeremiah," Aaron said, sitting down in the seat Dalia once occupied, "Getting some rest?"

Jeremiah looked up, making eye contact with the metallic man. He let out a half smile to meet Aarons full one, "I suppose so."

"Well, maybe it is a blessing, so don't treat it like a curse. I can't rest, I just reboot," He smiled again at Jeremiah, then he turned his attention to the window behind him, "But, we are almost there, so nothing we can do about it. Just don't worry too much, it clouds your mind." Before Jeremiah could respond, Aaron had made his way over to the ladder, climbing up to over watch.

He looked at his pack of cigarettes, *two left*. He contemplated lighting another one but turned his mind to the matters that awaited at the end of this drive. Tlaloc explained the situation; so much information crammed into Jeremiah's mind. It wasn't what he had expected of his life, yet nothing had been since the Grey swallowed him whole.

He nodded off for a moment, but quickly caught himself from falling asleep. He finally rose from the seat and walked up to the front of the bumpy rig.

"Dalia," He called out when he was within arm's reach of the driver's seat, "Any idea on how much longer till we get there?"

"Should be maybe another four hours," Her voice was full, unlike Jeremiah's sleep soaked vocal chords. Dalia obviously took note of the weariness in his voice, "Get back to the back, find a cot, and get some sleep until Xavier or Nathalie call you up top. No point in worrying about what's waiting."

"Are you sure?"

Dalia gave no answer, just a quick glance in the mirror that told Jeremiah everything he needed to know about where the conversation was heading. He stood slowly before making his way to the bunks of the rig. There, he found the solitude and sanctity of his mind in sleep.

The rig had parked, just on the outskirts of the track. Before them was a series of large hills, blocking their view as to what may be inside. Dalia had explained to Jeremiah that they had to wait to enter the track until everyone had been well rested, just in case something was to happen. That was hours ago, and now, Jeremiah lay awake in his bunk, as the rest of the crew inspected their gear; awaiting to enter the track.

Jeremiah had already completed his inspection of his own equipment long before the others awoke, and so he gathered his thoughts for the time being. He could hear Xavier complaining about this or that, Nathalie and Dalia remained silent even when the questions were directed at them. The rig seemed to be in a state of lost thoughts and meaningless disarray. Aaron had been left to keep watch, as all he needed to inspect he did through computer like processes. Jeremiah was still unsure as to how this worked, but understood that he couldn't possibly begin to comprehend what went on in the metal man's mind.

He felt a nudge at his side. He turned over to see Nathalie standing next to him, "Time to move out," She said, her eyes still heavy with sleep.

Jeremiah nodded and rolled out of his bunk, making his way over to the ladder to get to over watch. There, he saw Aaron, eating an apple towards the front of the rig. Once he had noticed Jeremiah, he shot him a quick comforting smile before looking out to the hills that they would soon be approaching. The rig roared to life beneath them, slowly rolling forward. Nathalie popped her head up through the hatch, calling out something to Aaron in French. Aaron acknowledged and Nathalie made her way up to over watch with them.

Aaron stood, walking over to Jeremiah accompanied by Nathalie. She extended a hand that held a single unlit cigarette. Jeremiah looked up at Nathalie, only to have Aaron speak for her, "It is a gift," He said, gesturing for Jeremiah to take the cigarette from her hand, "She couldn't think of the proper way to say it in English, so she had me translate. I believe she said; 'tell him that he should have a good smoke before we go in, not that crap he has.' It is the best translation I can offer."

Jeremiah took the cigarette, looking over at Nathalie. Before he could even think of a reply, he began to chuckle, causing Nathalie and Aaron to laugh with him.

Nathalie took a seat next to Jeremiah, lighting herself a cigarette as Jeremiah lit his. To him, her cigarette tasted just like any other cigarette that he had smoked since falling into the Grey. It made him miss his southern tobacco, hand rolled and sun dried. He wondered if that would be something that would await him on the other side.

He knew it was a strange thought to have; after all, he missed his family more than anything. But after seeing his son stand next to him, he tried to let his mind wander from his family. As much as this fight *was* about vengeance, it was also about what was right. He had to manage to stop Whisper, for any of the other families that could lose a loved one thanks to her insanity. Still, the thoughts of death were not the thoughts to be having just before facing a God.

Nathalie sat in silence next to him, the rigs movements causing her to sway slightly as she gazed off into the distance behind her cigarette. From what Jeremiah could imagine, she was praying without moving her lips.

The track finally appeared on the other side of the hills. Jeremiah stood, taking in the twists and turns of the track, the decrepit buildings. He tried to pinpoint anything that may give away the location of Whisper, but everything about the track seemed to be in slow decay; all except a blue-green lake in the middle with a small building on an island.

The rig slowed to a stop at a small barricade just outside of the black tarmac. The crew disembarked, slowly creeping closer and closer to the gate that separated them from entering the track. First Aaron slipped through the chained fence, followed by Xavier, then Nathalie. Before Jeremiah could make his way under the chain, Dalia stopped him with a hand to his chest. Her eyes looked slightly concerned, her jaw clenched shut. She gave him a reassuring nod before allowing him to continue on.

Beyond the gate was pavement littered with vehicles and debris. Jeremiah crept past multiple crashed vehicles, noting the writing on their sides. It didn't take him long to realize that some of the markings on the vehicles indicated someone's name and country.

P. Takahara next to the white flag with a red Circle inside of it. The vehicle was overturned, and a gold cross was displayed at the front and back of it.

Another vehicle with the same gold cross had the name *T. Jarvis* with what appeared to be an American flag next to it. The Vehicle also had *CHEVROLET SS* written in large bold letters at the bottom of the vehicle.

A Scottish flag with the name *C. Kapricorn* was on the side of a vehicle that was named after a horse, it even had one depicted on the side. Inside of the vehicle, Jeremiah noted a driver behind the wheel, his body beginning to decay, limp against the seat. He made a cross with his hand as he passed, hoping that whatever peace was to be had, that soul would have it.

Finally, he found his feet side by side with the others of the crew at the shore of the small lake in the middle of the track. They looked out over the water, off toward the small pristine building.

"Well," Jeremiah said under his breath, "Guess this is it," His knees felt weak, his hands had a slight tremble as he rubbed them against his pant legs to relieve the sweat from the palms. He had to be prepared for whatever may lay within the small building. Something caught his eye on the other side of the lake. There, among the duckweed and tall grass was a heron making its way towards the water's edge. Jeremiah felt as if it were looking at him as it walked.

"Are you ready?" Xavier asked.

"Sure as hell hope so," Jeremiah responded.

"Alright," Dalia said, pulling her handgun from her holster, "After you, cowboy."

CHAPTER 24

Jeremiah found a small walkway leading to the island that was constructed of land and stone. It turned the island more into a peninsula, but he wondered if that would be the best way to enter the unknown structure. Finally, he concluded that he must wade through the blue water.

He stepped his first foot into the water. It was cold as anything he had experienced, seeping through his trousers and onto his skin. He shivered but continued on his path to the building. Luckily for him, it seemed to only be about five or six meters of water to wade across. He took his rifle from his back and shouldered it, just in case it was to get deep enough to get anything into the barrel.

The wade across the water seemed to be much shorter than it actually was, partially thanks to the fact that the water never made it past knee height. Thanks to this, he could move much quicker than he had originally intended; however, it brought on the problem of noise. Still, once his feet reached dry land on the other side, he laid down, his chest flat against the ground.

He wanted to hide from anyone who may come outside looking for him, yet after roughly fifteen minutes of waiting for some enemy footsteps, no one had exited the small structure. He turned back to the shoreline from where he departed, scanning every inch of it to be sure the crew had dispersed to their appropriate locations. Due to what Dalia called "safety reasons", Jeremiah had been left in the dark about what their plans may be. Still, he felt as though she was right when it came to the best interests of her crew, yet it was disheartening being unable to pinpoint their locations.

Finally, he rose up from the banks in a crouch, stepping silently among the tall grass and shrubbery. He maintained the crouch as he circled the building, attempting to find an entrance around its yellow brick structure. It was a simple building; four walls, two windows on the sides, and one door at the front where the land bridge had been constructed.

Its door was red, painted long ago by the looks of it as it had faded to almost pink. There were scratches exposing bare metal at all four corners, the knob of the same color as the exposed metal. He stood there a moment, hesitating to turn the nob and enter. Still, he knew that the longer he lingered outside, the more he could dwell on what lay beyond its barrier.

He placed his hand on the door knob, it's cold steel infecting his palm and fingers. It turned with the cracking of decaying and rusted metal. With a screech and a click, the knob turned as far as possible, allowing Jeremiah to push open the door with the utmost of ease. It glided silently on its hinges, exposing a bare stone room inside.

Jeremiah let out a sigh of disappointment; the room was empty, without a person or Goddess in sight. His knees shook so violently he felt that he would collapse from the pain his soul had to bare thanks to the vacant room. As he moved his body down to a knee, he noticed a small crawl space leading downward at the furthest wall from the entrance. It was small enough to not be hidden, but as he approached, he noticed that the rooms floor had a slight slope, allowing him to realize that it was a full doorway with stairs that led into a hollow space beneath the island. He took a quick look at his surroundings before finding his footing on the first step of the long staircase down.

The staircase seemed to have been lit on its own accord, illuminating the walls with a brilliant white. Jeremiah could not place what type of stone flanked both of his sides, yet it wasn't much care to him. He only knew that he would need to find Whisper in the structure below, and he intended to make it her tomb.

The room beneath the island was large; much larger than the lake, yet smaller than the track. From what he could tell it had more than one entrance, yet could not pinpoint exactly what structures on the surface they led to. However, that was not his concern; for there, in the center of the room, stood Whisper with her back to him. He thought about taking aim with his rifle for a moment, yet decided against it as it had not worked the times prior.

Her head was bowed, as if in prayer over some object that was blocked by her body from Jeremiah's view. He had gathered his thoughts quickly and said a small prayer to God before he took another step inside of the room.

"Well," He said, slinging his rifle to his back, "If it isn't the *new* god."

Whisper whipped around, her ice blue hair waving by the force of her sudden turn. Her violet eyes were wide; not in horror, more in shocked surprise. Her lips quivered before speaking, "Jeremiah. And how did you gain entrance without my knowledge?"

"I have someone on the inside if ya' must know. Honestly, I came here, lookin' for some sorta' vengeance and whatnot," He began to pace the perimeter of the bunker, making sure Whisper's eyes followed him, "But I figured out somethin' about you. Made my heart weep a lil'; not by much, but just enough." He stopped near one of the other entrances, running his fingers along the corners of the large cut stones.

"Oh," Whisper replied, stepping forward toward Jeremiah. Behind her was a small altar with a small gunmetal colored stone atop it, "And just who might that be?"

Jeremiah could tell by her body posture that she was more shocked than afraid still. He took a deep breath, pulling his hand towards the hilt of his knife, "Doesn't matter. Let's just say I know a lot more about you now; a hell of a lot more than I did."

Whisper took another step toward Jeremiah, her jade dress rubbing against her legs. Jeremiah tried to not pay attention to her body, averting his eyes off to the right. There, he saw a humanoid figure creeping in through one of the entrances.

It was Aaron.

"So, what do you know?" She queried.

"Well, Chalchiuhtlicue," Her eyes grew wide as he spoke her true name, "Still, I prefer callin' ya' *Whisper*. Anyway, your husband is not that happy 'bout your damn antics going on," Jeremiah wanted to nod toward the stone on the altar, but he knew he would have exposed Aaron in doing so, "And he told me all about Tecciztecatl. And, honestly, you two have the longest damn names ever."

Whisper snarled at Jeremiah, and then turned her attention to the stone on the altar; She caught sight of Aaron creeping along the wall. Aaron froze, then presented a half-hearted apologetic smile to Whisper. "You *FOOLS!*" She called out, holding out both hands as if to strangle the pair.

Jeremiah fell to his knees, water spurted forth from his mouth.

He was drowning.

He looked up, Whisper standing with the same posture, her eyes looked almost red from his perspective on the ground. He noticed she was only paying attention to him and she didn't notice Aaron creeping up slowly from behind her. Although she had obviously used the same witchcraft on both of them, it somehow didn't affect the half-metal man.

Aaron reached his metallic hand, its gears whirling and turning, grabbing Whisper by the arm, turning her to face him. Jeremiah felt the water exit his lungs as soon as the other metallic hand connected with Whisper's abdomen. Jeremiah coughed, covering his mouth with one hand as his other arm pressed against his chest. He couldn't bring himself to his feet, he just felt as if he didn't have the strength.

His eyes were blurred with the pain as he tried to watch Aaron.

Whisper was no longer doubled over in pain, instead, she was standing toe to toe with Aaron. His hand was still firmly grasping her arm as they stood there. She took her hands, placing her palms against the temples of Aaron.

Aaron let out a painful scream as he grasped at her wrists, attempting to pull her hands away. Soon, the scream turned to a gargle, sparks began to fly from all metallic parts of his body as water spewed out of every opening.

"You ignorant little man!" Whisper called out, her hands still pressed firmly to his head as he struggled. Water covered her from the waist down as it spewed forth onto her body, "You think you can face a *god*!"

Aaron's head began to spasm, his fingers and hands twitching while remaining a tight grip on Whispers wrists. Jeremiah found his footing, attempting to unsheathe his knife. He noticed Aaron's eyes drew to his, a smile twinkled within them.

"I-I-I-I-I do!" Aaron called out, his twitches affecting his speech, "I am to-to-to-to-to-to watch-ch-ch you fall. Fall from grace, and-d-d-d-d-d-d..." the sound of a record coming to a halt came from his mouth. Aaron could not find the last words before the whirl of his movements became a hiss. He fell to the ground, his life slowly seemed to dim from his eyes just before they shut.

Whisper was panting as she brushed her arms clean of the oil that had been spilled from Aaron's hands. She turned to find Jeremiah, standing only a few feet from her.

Jeremiah had his knife in his hand, his chest heaved up and down as he stood facing the murderess. She panted before she began to chuckle, "Jeremiah Washington, you come here to slay me? 'Slay the beast'? But, honestly, am I really the one who deserves it?"

She waved her hand, and next to Jeremiah stood Bobby once more. Bobby looked up to his father, eyes wide, his perfect little smile on his face. Jeremiah looked down at his son, a tear dropped from his eye.

"Look at the eyes of your child, was it really his time to go?" She took a step closer to the two, "After all, I am not the evil one. I offered your son a spot amongst the Gods; he would have been a god of his own. He would have been all knowing, all powerful, able to change the tides and rains. *You* killed him, *you* took his possibility of being immortal."

She gestured with a single open palm down to the small transparent child. Jeremiah didn't look down; he couldn't look down at *his* child again. Fortunately for him, he was already able to hear what bobby had to say, all thanks to Tlaloc. He was also able to make peace with the fact that he had not been the reason his child had gone mad; he had not been the reason a bullet was the only escape. No, it was not him, it was all doings of a broken hearted mother.

"I know why ya' did it," Jeremiah began, his eyes fixed on Whisper as his child looked up to him, "Hell, what mother wouldn't do anything to have her kid again. What *father* wouldn't do the same? I ain't got a thing against your boy, ain't got a thing against your husband. I got problems with *you* takin my family from me.

"Hell, I wish I could see 'em again," He looked down to Bobby. He could tell there were tears welling up in his small son's eyes, "But, I don't have no intentions of killin' another man for that. I say I'd rip the world apart for 'em, but I couldn't take someone else's family. It's a damn hard line.

"Tlaloc told me about how you went mad, delusional, ya' just up and left. He told me how ya searched far and wide for that rock; for that little piece of y'alls son. But really, do ya' think he'd want that? Do ya' think that Tecciztecatl would want ya' to take the life of those innocent people? To hell he would."

Whisper shot Jeremiah a look that could simultaneously melt lead while freezing water. She glanced quickly over her shoulder to the rock before turning back. Jeremiah had begun to take steps forward, his knife moving from hand to hand slowly as he walked forward. She lifted a hand to bring him to his knees once more, but Bobby bolted in between them. Her witchcraft was ineffective against the child's spirit. It gave Jeremiah just the time he needed.

Jeremiah lurched forward, his knife out in front of him. He passed through his child's body, his knife cutting into Whispers outstretched arm. She recoiled in pain, yet he was already on the attack once more, thrusting the knife toward her heart. She sidestepped, avoiding the blade by millimeters. However, her step to the side had an unfortunate consequence.

The altar that held the small silver rock quaked as Whisper knocked her heel against it. It wobbled, tilting from side to side. The

181

stone slid from the altar on one of its tilts, crashing against the cold concrete floor.

The stone shattered.

Whisper let out a cry. She shrieked as tears ran down the scars on her face, scrambling over to the stone she attempted to put it back together. She caught Jeremiah from the corner of her eye, "YOU! *YOU!* You killed *my* son! I will rip you from this reality!"

She lunged forward, hands outstretched, reaching for Jeremiah's throat. They clamped down onto his neck, causing his eyes to bulge slightly at the new pressure she exerted on him. She blinked, her facial expression went from rage to confusion. Both Jeremiahs and Whispers eyes wandered down. Jeremiah's blade had met its mark, penetrating perfectly into her heart – or more where a heart should be.

Jeremiah's eyes closed.

CHAPTER 25

Jeremiah recognized the white nothingness. It was as a dream had once been; a dream where Marie had appeared to him. He looked around, trying to find something familiar to grasp onto, trying to hear any voice he could, any scent.

It was Silent.

Jeremiah broke down into tears.

He felt that he had failed in what he was meant to do, he was banned to purgatory. He sat in the vast nothingness, counting his sins in his head as he repeated the Hail Mary prayer over and over out loud. Something had to come from being locked in purgatory, there had to be some way to get in his light so that he could once more hold his beloved Jennifer. He closed his eyes, burying his head in his hands as his elbows rested on his knees.

"Jeremiah," A vaguely familiar voice said. He opened his eyes to see tan legs tattooed in blue swirls before him, "I am very sorry," Jeremiah looked up to see Tlaloc's outstretched hand, beckoning Jeremiah to take it.

"Well, what in the Hell happened?" Jeremiah asked as he took Tlaloc's hand.

Tlaloc helped him to his feet, "You confronted my wife, you saved her from herself. You saved her from her absolute infatuation with bringing our child back. As I said, she searched far and wide for a single moon rock to bring his spirit back into our world." Tlaloc began to walk off into the nothingness.

"I know," Jeremiah jogged after him, attempting to keep pace with the massive figure, "I'm sorry that the stone got a bit broken in all that."

"Sorry? That was the one thing she never thought of; that I never thought of. She ran about, going mad with the love of our child, attempting to bring him back into this world. Neither one of us ever thought that breaking the stone would release our poor son from his minuscule tomb of eternity."

Jeremiah blinked, puzzled at what he meant, "Yeah?"

"Yes. Thanks to you, our son is once more looking down on the world. He brings the tides, bringing the surf to the land. He is once more flying high in the sky. Though the mist attempts to block his view, he

finds a way."

Jeremiah still had no way of responding, yet he continued to keep pace with Tlaloc as they strode through the nothingness. His head swam with a million more questions than he knew no entity could answer. Still, there was something comforting in the stroll with Tlaloc, even if his answers would never be answered.

He turned to Tlaloc, ready to ask just one simple question, yet the world around him began to swirl before a single word could escape him.

Dalia had brought the remains of her crew member up from the bunker. Aaron was always a good man, always willing to do what was best for the team. Now, here he was, a jumble of limbs and electronic bits. Rust had appeared throughout all of his metallic components, burns at almost every electronic connection.

Aside from Aarons body and a small pile of dust on the ground next to a fallen altar, the room had been completely emptied. Nathalie, Xavier, and herself had searched the track for a few hours for any signs of Jeremiah or Whisper. Unfortunately, there was no sign of anyone – god or otherwise – anywhere near the track.

Xavier sat behind the wheel of the rig as Dalia brought Aarons body aboard. She had never seen Xavier so somber, but had the exact same feeling.

"Let's set off," She said over her shoulder as she walked toward the back of the rig.

"Where we off to?" Xavier asked, just barely loud enough for Dalia to hear. She could feel a hint of sadness in his voice; he was obviously trying to cover it up.

"We should head back to Tlaloc," She had paused halfway down the rig, "At least we can tell him what we know."

Xavier nodded as the rig roared to life. As the rig began to move forward, Dalia lay Aarons remains down in his empty bunk. She stood a moment, lingering above his body. She wanted to say a prayer, she wanted to say something that could help her make sense of everything, yet nothing came to mind.

She continued to the back for the washroom. Nathalie reclined in one of the rearmost seats, smoking a cigarette, staring out the window.

"Nathalie," Dalia said as she approached. Once she had been

acknowledged, she placed a hand on her shoulder, "Need someone up on overwatch. I'll be up in a second to lend a hand."

Nathalie gave her a blank look, a tear just kissing her cheek. Still, she rose up to her feet and began to make her way over to the ladder.

"Nathalie,"

"Yeah?"

"I miss him too, but let's get back in one piece."

She watched Nathalie disappear up the ladder before she opened the door to the small washroom at the back of the bus. Once the door had latched, she sat down on the latrine, burying her face into her palms. She began to cry.

She prayed for everything to be alright, for everything to go back to the way it was before the Grey sucked her in. She knew it was no use, but still she found some comfort in the idea of a higher being listening. She couldn't stop herself from the thought, she couldn't stop herself from the stream of tears that caused her to hide from her crew.

She had to be the strong one.

She lifted her head, looking out the small window. Her eyes grew wide. Outside the window, in the sky, she could see the moon – just barely – through the mist.

She smiled to herself; Aaron had not died in vein.

Jeremiah's eyes began to open; the white nothingness had subsided to a memory at that moment. A familiar scent of clementine's infected his nostrils as he attempted to wipe the weariness from his eyes. The bed he was in was warm and comforting, the sheets pulled up to his shoulders. He looked around the room, trying to make everything come back into focus.

Familiar – albeit out of focus – paintings hung cleanly and scattered among the walls. He lifted himself up in the bed, propping his back against the wall. His chest and side were in excruciating pain, his throat throbbing. He turned and rubbed his eyes.

There, on the table next to him was a glass of tea. As he reached for it a familiar voice called his name. He smiled to himself before turning to face Alexis who stood at the door. In her hands was another glass of tea and a pack of cigarettes. She had a green and blue pillow tucked under her arm.

"You... You woke up," She stuttered, rushing to his side to embrace him, "They found you, face down in the dirt just outside the gate. Where have you been, why did you leave?" She sniffled, whipping mucus from her nose.

"I'm, I'm sorry."

"No, you can't just be sorry. Please, just tell me where you were."

Jeremiah looked her in the eye, his mind racing with everything that had happened to him in his life. He wanted to gather the words to explain to Alexis why he had up and left, but his mind just couldn't find anything; still he spoke a few simple words, "The moon."

Alexis smiled at Jeremiah, and he felt the warmth radiating from her. In that smile and warmth, he could feel the love of his Jennifer as she beckoned for him to take the next step in his life.

B.E. Amestoy

Jeramiah Wash

That mist. Oh, that terrible mist. It took it all away from me. I suppose I am a fool, the lonely cowboy that rides to chaos.

Riding to find a way home...

I remember what it was like before all this; the sweet smell of Jenny, the laughter of my boy.

You ever been to Texas? That, right there, is the Promised Land. Perfectly crafted by God himself. Blue skies, low rolling green and brown hills. Oh, finding myself there; you can't even think without findin' some beauty. That's where I posted myself; 300 acres of Texas prairie. I had good cattle, nice little house, a chicken coop right out back. Bobby (my son), well he'd wake up with his daddy every mornin', just so he could feed the chickens.

Then, the mist came...

I was out mending a fence, out there in the hills. My horse ended up getting spooked. Well, I tried to calm her, then the sun was gone... Just gone... I turned and watched that smoke leak out and descend on my land. It ate the hills, the cattle, everything. I tried to mount my horse, but she bucked me right off.

That was the last thing I remember before I blacked out.

So, there I was; alone and in the breath of Satan himself. My right leg must've caught some bit of the barbed wire, 'cause I was bleedin' something fierce. Patched up my leg and started my way home. All the beauty I came to know was gone; not even the grass seemed to escape the demons grasp; it sunk me so low. Must've walked about an hour before I found my home. Out front I found my horse ripped to shreds. Looked a lot like a pack of wolves had a feast on her. Poor girl...

My fears grew; the front door was torn clean off.

I rushed myself in, and I swear you could just smell the blood and death. Heard some sort of roarin' overhead; made me drop down to my knees and cover my ears, clenching my eyes shut. What fuckin' madness was this?

When I could move again, I slowly made my way into the kitchen, only to find my son's back to me. He was knelt over the torn and dismembered remains of my beloved Jenny. I couldn't speak, just held my mouth. I moved closer; fighting tears for the sake of my little boy. I finally found myself close enough to pat his back.

As soon as my hand touched him, he whipped around. Eyes red and without soul; no whites, no pupils, and my wife's blood coming out through the teeth of a grin the devil himself would shit himself if he saw it. Before I knew anything he took a chunk outa my leg. I fell back to see my blood spill out on the floor. A shriek of a million witches came out of that boy's mouth.

Then he just attacked his daddy.

I wrestled with him when he lunged at me again, keeping his teeth away from me, screaming. I eventually got a hold of my rifle and he caught a bullet between his eyes.

I cried... I cried for days...

Made in the USA
Middletown, DE
30 July 2022

70190707R00116